T0209852

Tale of Teary Isles

Beauty in the Shattered

SPECIAL EDITION

P. DUTTON

WestBow
PRESS®
A DIVISION OF THOMAS NELSON
& ZONDERVAN

WestBow Press books may be ordered through booksellers or by contacting:

WestBow Press
A Division of Thomas Nelson & Zondervan
1663 Liberty Drive
Bloomington, IN 47403
www.westbowpress.com
844-714-3454

Scripture taken from the King James Version of the Bible.

ISBN: 978-1-6642-4124-4 (sc)
ISBN: 978-1-6642-4123-7 (hc)
ISBN: 978-1-6642-4125-1 (e)

Library of Congress Control Number: 2021915045

Print information available on the last page.

WestBow Press rev. date: 08/05/2021

Dedicated to—

My mom and dad. They have ever been my biggest fans, supporters, and pillars for advice when I am uncertain. I can never fully express how fortunate or grateful I am to have been blessed with such amazing parents.

They endowed me with a strong foundation in faith, because without it I know for certain that I would never be the person I am today.

Thank you, mom and dad, this is for you both.

Contents

PART 2

Part 1

Behold, we count them happy which endure.
Ye have heard of the patience of Job....'

JAMES 5:11

Chapter

1

ELLA METSULA HAD KNOWN THE LIFE OF A SLAVE since the young age of ten. When she was just four years-old a terrible plague swept through her home village in the kingdom of Millet. This plague wiped out over half the population of the kingdom, including Della's parents.

This plague was significantly hard on Millet because of its economical position in Vararmor. Millet was in the desert region near the Forest of the Unknown and offered little for land to grow crops, because it was arid and hot most of the year.

Due to this, the kingdom of Millet's economy was based on fishing and relied heavily upon the trade of slavery for survival and with the plague the kingdom struggled to bounce back from the tragedy.

Shortly after their passing, Della was sent to live with her grandmother in a neighboring village. Her grandmother was a cold, cruel callous lady who was only concerned with her own personal interest and saw Della as only a burden on her.

Being the mother of Della's father, she made it known that she never approved of the marriage of Della's parents. In fact, she blamed Della's mother for her son dying from the plague and was angry for them dropping their child in her lap.

Adding to her grandmother's resentment towards her, was the fact that Della so closely resembled her mother and for it, her grandmother despised her. Della had her mother's complexion of dark brown and a shapely narrow face and wavy thick black hair and gentle fawn-eyes.

Her grandmother was a very lazy woman who never worked and spent much of her time at the tavern down the road drinking. She would loan Della out to the other villagers around them. Della had to do tasks such as helping clean houses, cook, wash, and watch over other children while their parents were away at work.

Whatever Della earned from completing these tasks, her grandmother would take and spend on ale at the tavern. She left nothing for Della to buy food or clothes for herself. A few of the families that Della worked for would send her home with a little food and some of the village women made her clothes when she needed them.

When her grandmother was at home, Della didn't know a moment of peace because she was worked constantly and often beaten. Things carried on like this for Della for the next six years, until the coin grew short and tasks for Della were fewer.

Desperate for drinking coin, her grandmother dragged Della to the market square to the slaver's market and sold her. With twenty-six coppers in hand, her grandmother walked away from the pleading sobbing child and left her in the hands of her new masters, never looking back.

Della had been purchased by the head-cook of the noble family of Millet to be a kitchen maid along with a handful of other girls. Della and the other girls had the tasks of clearing the table of the royal family, washing dishes, going to the market to collect goods, and cleaning the kitchen every evening after mealtimes.

The Head Maid was Brunella, a stiff, icy old woman, with a hard face and a firm hand that she used freely on the kitchen girls. If Brunella did not like a certain kitchen girl she made it known by being brutally cruel to her, working her harder than the others and beating her for no reason.

Della learned early on to do her tasks quickly and efficiently, but most of all she learned to keep her mouth shut. A kitchen girl who spoke too much or got smart with anyone in authority; would certainly feel the wrath of Brunella.

Della would get up before dawn every morning and worked very late into the night, her only meal was table scraps from the noble family, though, Della got whatever all the other kitchen staff didn't eat. Which usually wasn't enough.

She had no room to go to or a bed to sleep on, but would curl up on the flour sacks beside one of the large stoves and slept there. She did her tasks well enough that Brunella would send her out to the market to gathered goods for the kitchen, which provided Della with a glimpse of the outside world.

Della got to see the world and life that she would never be a part of. She loved being allowed to get out of the kitchen, but it was torture to see how happy and free everyone else was.

She would often marvel at how carefree the other women were as they passed through the streets, either with a handsome gentlemen or maidens as they went around buying goods. The women had neatly comb hair adorned with all manners of jewelry, ivory combs, and chains. Some of their hair was half pinned up on their heads, while others wore their hair loose and wavy.

Some slaves belonging to a wealthy family or one of the noblemen's house servants wore golden or silver rings in their ears to demonstrate that they belonged to a family of high-born people.

Most of these well-dressed people were allowed to come and go as they pleased, they never seemed to be worried or in a rush. Della knew that if Brunella assumed the young girl was absent for too long she would most certainly be beaten, therefore, she could not linger too long in the market.

Della had been too young to remember what it was like to be free to do as you chose, because she had been so young when her parents died. But, she felt that it must have been good, something special.

Della was able to carry on with her daily duties for the next four years. Over time, due to the lack of food and long exhausting hours, she became too thin and weakly to keep up with her workload.

Brunella soon became unhappy with the results of her work and she sent the young woman to the slaver's market during the kingdom festival. Here, hundreds of young men, women, and children were placed on a crate in the center of the market square and sold off one by one, like they were nothing more than cattle.

Della and a group of other young women were bought by a man of a shifty countenance.

He was tall and thin, appearing to be in his later thirties with a dark complexion, black hair and a thin moustache. His dark eyes were narrow and reflected an untrustworthiness about them. His voice was soft and slightly accented; he was sure to overexaggerate his movements and use eloquent words when he spoke to others.

When he paid for the girls, he used golden coinage which suggested that either he himself was wealthy or that he was from a titled household. Either way, it garnered him respect and stares of awe from the nearby spectators He brought them to a great white house on the outskirts of the main city. The house had a thatched roof and the shutters of the windows were painted a bright red.

A beautiful woman with a delicate build, honey-yellow curly hair, and baby blue-eyes stood in the doorway of the house ready to greet the newcomers. Though her hair was finely combed, and her face a soft as the coat of a newborn lamb, her hands were rough and lined from years of hard labor. Warmly, she welcomed each new girl to their new home, with a gentle smile and a kind word.

There was an expression of sorrow deep in her eyes as she watched each girl file past her into the great house.

"These girls are your responsibility, Mauda. Do what you are able with them." he ordered in a dismal tone as he frowned at the girls. "Some are in such a terrible state…what a pity."

Mauda only nodded, giving a tight smile.

"Well, you have six months to make a difference." the Master said pulling a large pouch from his belt and held it out to her. "This should cover any expenses they may incur."

Without another word, the nameless man turned on his heels and briskly strode out of the house slamming the door behind him.

Mauda was sweet and kindly towards the women. She gave them each gentle words of encouragement as she bathed and dressed them in their new clothes and fed them. She was certain to give each girl individual attention, teaching them good table manners, proper etiquette, and how to conduct themselves as ladies.

Within four months, Della was able to gain a healthy weight, her skin complexion darkened, and she matured into a full beautiful young woman of fifteen-years-old. She refined her speaking skills, how to behave at the table during mealtimes, and how to curtsey before those of higher social standing.

None of the girls knew why they were brought to the great house or what purpose their master had bought them for. They were mystified as to why they were being treated so well; being fed the finest delicacies, wearing excellent quality clothing, and allowed to attend some of the social engagements in the village. Della was slowly growing suspicious as to why so much care and attention was put toward their personal beauty and manners.

She had befriended Mauda and felt comfortable enough with the older woman, that she felt she could trust her. Often, Della would question her about what their master's true intentions were for them. Mauda would always dodge around her repeated inquires, but Della noted that the older woman would become somber and fearful whenever she was asked at what their master wanted with them.

"Della, aren't you ready?" Mauda asked coming into the bathing room carrying fresh linens.

Della was finishing dressing after her bath when Mauda walked in.

Mauda announced to the girls that there was going to be a high-society party that evening, and they were invited. Since that afternoon Mauda had each girl bathe, dress their hair, and outfitted them in the finest clothing.

Della purposely waited to be the last girl to bathe and dress up, in reality, she wasn't at all interested in going to another engagement. She was tired of countless men looking her up and down, poking her and touching her hair. She knew there was something very unnatural about their behavior.

"No," Della sighed deeply as she patted her hair dry.

"Why not, dear?" Mauda sweetly inquired.

The older woman set her basket aside and came over to Della and sat down on the edge of the wash tub beside her.

"I don't wish to go." Della confessed.

"Oh?" Mauda gave her full attention.

"I don't like these engagements. The way the men look at us, touch our hair, poking at us, or wanting us alone at their tables." Della explained frowning in distaste.

"But it is a great honor to be a guest at a noble gentlemen's table." Mauda reasoned.

"It does not feel so,"

"Della, being a well-mannered lady is very important to your future. If you are able to catch the fancy of any one of these men, they could ask for your hand in marriage or perhaps you might serve in their house," the older woman pressed earnestly. "You should not look unfavorably upon these opportunities."

"Opportunities? What opportunity is there in serving as a maid?" Della felt defiance rise in her chest. "I have been a servant all my life and there is no opportunity there."

"Della," Mauda's tone became sweet. "You must not look upon the positions offered by these men unfavorably. It would provide you with a sure place in society instead of what the master has in mind for you."

"And what does the master have in mind?" Della was quick to counter.

Mauda seemed to realize her folly, her cheeks went flush, and eyes widened with fear.

"Mauda, tell me. What does the master have in mind for us?"

"Look," Mauda dismissively shook her head. "Why don't you get dressed and I'll help you with your hair before the party. Ok?"

Della noticed that the older woman had become anxious and all out of sorts at Della's inquiry. Della knew that Mauda was hiding something, it was enough to strike terror into the poor woman.

"But Mauda," Della pleaded looking into the other woman's face searching for understanding.

"You can tell me what the master wants with us. We are friends, be reassured that I will tell no one."

"No," Mauda stated firmly as she stood.

"Mauda—"

"No, Della, no!" the older woman snapped shortly.

"Now that is enough! Dress quickly, we are expected to be there in an hour."

Without so much as a look, Mauda turned her back to Della, the older woman brought a hand to her face and rushed from the room. Della felt a stab of guilt, she knew that she hurt and upset Mauda with her repeated inquiries.

Despite this, she wanted to know what awaited them at the end of the six months and why it had such a terrible effect on poor Mauda.

As the end of the six months was drawing near; Mauda's mood was clouded over with a deep graveness. Della couldn't fathom how anyone could be unhappy when they were allowed free access to all the food, clothing, and social parties as they were.

Mauda was put in such a depressed frame of mind that some days she refused to emerge from her room, leaving the girls to look after themselves. Out of curiosity on one of these days, Della decided to try the front door and see if they could go out freely.

It was locked.

This was the second sign to Della that something wasn't right about them being here. Many of the girls had come to rely heavily on

Mauda's special care that they did not know how do perform general tasks for themselves.

Cooking, cleaning, and mending were some of the things that Mauda neglected to teach the girls. Therefore, Della took up these tasks because of her experience. Clothes were brought to her to be mended, she cooked meals for the girls, and tidied the house.

The girls began to look to her like a tutor and trusted confidant. Even with Mauda around, Della began to help out by assisting the other girls with their baths, helping them dress and even took a little time to teach them to read.

After some of the social engagements, girls would come to her that had been cruelly mistreated or made public mockery of by the men and women at these parties. They would pour out to her their sorrows, disappointments, fear, and hopes. Della comforted them and tried to give what little encouragement she could to them.

One fateful day, the girls discovered the master's intentions for them.

The master showed up at the end of the six months, only he didn't come alone. He was accompanied by four Crimson Knights of the kingdom of Aclestis. These knights wore bright silver chest plates, with the engraving of a snarling wolf's head on them. Under their chest plates they wore chainmail, heavy gauntlets, long blood-red cloaks, at their sides hung broad swords, and tucked under one arm was a silver visor helmet shaped as a snarling wolf head.

To Della they were utterly terrifying. She knew the other girls were filled with the same terror at the sight of the men, but she masked her fear and appeared confident before them. She knew that if she appeared calm and collected, that it would help the other girls.

When they arrived at the great house, the master ordered that all the girls be brought out into the large center room and line up before the knight's for inspection.

Trembling in fear, most of the girls gathered near Della for protection as the knights began to look them over. The young women's hair was pulled, they were roughly poked, prodded, and their teeth were checked. As this was done the girls began breaking into tears understanding fully what was happening to them.

The knights handled each girl like they were livestock.

"Very well," the burly lead knight announced when they were finished. "We'll take them all."

"Good, good," the master said greedily rubbing his hands together. "The price?"

"Two hundred pieces—in gold." the leader replied.

"G—gold?" the master stammered his eyes widening for a moment.

"They are fine, beautiful girls and my men tend to grow restless on the campaign trail," the knight explained with a cruel grin. "They need excitement and entertainment. Which these fine creatures will provide."

"Agreed!" the master declared eagerly.

The exchange of coin passed between the men and to seal the deal they struck each other's hand roughly before bowing their heads. Moments later, three of the knights came for the girls. They whimpered and sobbed in fright as they were pulled and shoved toward the door of the great house.

All Della's trust and hopes were shattered at that very instance; and the woman she called friend only stood by and watched as the girls were sold off. Mauda had a chance to save herself and all the girls at any time in those past six months, but she never took it.

Della knew that she and the other women were bound for the worst kind of enslavement in existence. They were to be camp wenches—entertainment for lonely horrid soldiers.

My life is over, Della resignedly told herself as she and the other women were shuffled out of the great house and into an enclosed wagon to be carted off to their new masters.

To their doom.

Della was shuffle around in the army camp like a common piece of waste. She never gave into the advances of the men and fought against them like a wild cat. Quickly, the soldiers grew tired of how difficult she was and eventually gave up trying to bed her.

Instead, they decided to make sport of Della by shoving her around between groups of soldiers. They beat and abusively tossed her around from man to man; to them she had no value, but to be continuously punished.

Della was fair game for any amount of abuse a soldier wished to inflict on her, and she suffered this way for the next three and a half brutally long years. In those years, she saw other girls, friends and strangers alike come and go.

She did her best to care for them, but there was little she could do when the soldiers came for them nearly every night. She bore witness to the torment and cruelty inflicted on these girls until she thought she could bear it no more.

She promised herself that if ever she got the chance to lay hands on a weapon, she would defend these girls against the soldiers and knights vicious attacks or die trying.

Chapter

2

"VICTORY NEVER FELT SO GOOD," A YOUNG SOLDIER remarked.

Looking over his shoulder he caught sight of the knight standing behind him and added sheepishly.

"If you don't mind my saying so, Sir."

"Couldn't agree more." the knight said with a pleasant grin.

"Where should we start on the spoils, Sir?" the soldier inquired sounding overwhelmed.

"Anywhere." the knight said letting out a sighing breath.

The remains of the Varamorean army was a mess of strewn about belongings and bodies. There were a few stragglers from the assaulting army from the kingdom that were fleeing on their way back to Vararmor after being soundly beat by the army of Oak Land. It would take a few days to go through all of the remnants of the battle ground where all the valuables would be collected, and the bodies would be piled up to be burned.

"We should start with the dead," the soldier announced decidedly. "They will begin to rot and smell soon."

"Good choice." the knight complimented before he turned in a semi-circle to survey the ruins of the enemy encampment.

The injury that he had received to his waistline was really beginning to smart now that he was standing still. It was very noticeable now that the excitement of the battle had ebbed away and the weariness and exhaustion of the past few days was beginning to set in.

I could use a break right about now. the knight mused.

On the battle ground, discarded weaponry, fallen knights and soldiers alike littered the smoldering field. A few banners from both armies were haphazardly stuck into the earth, some were still being clutched by their dead bearers.

The sight of battle aftermath always brought the knight such deep sorrow and regret, it was the one thing he wished could be abolished from this world. War and killing never seemed to resolve much, it only left parents childless and made mourners of lovers and the wedded.

It will make mourns of many for the weeks and years to come…on both sides, he gave a heaving sigh, exhausting was seeping into his bones.

I wonder where Toby has gotten off to. he wondered as he began to work the buckles loose on the breast plate of his armor.

I could really use getting this heavy armor off and settling down for a long nap, right about now.

"Sir Almas! Sir Almas!"

A soldier came dashing breathlessly across the field over to where the knight was standing. The knight faced the soldier and gave a weary salute as the soldier stopped before him.

"Sir…" the young man gasped for breath as he gave a salute.

"Slow down, Adam." he told the young man as he held his hands up motioning to him.

The soldier slightly relaxed as he nodded and sucked in a deep breath.

"All right, go on." Sir Almas encouraged after a moment.

"Sir, I need you to come quick." the soldier explained as he shifted from one foot to the other.

"The men…we discovered a tent of young women."

"Women?" the knight uttered slightly surprised and puzzled.

"Yes, sir." the soldier confirmed with a foolish grin. "A handful of them. We tried to approach them in a friendly way, but…well."

"Well, what?" the knight probed.

"There's one of the women; she's got a dagger and she tries to attack anyone who comes near their tent. She attacked Thom and sliced his shoulder pretty good, but he managed to get away from her before she was able to do serious damage."

"We didn't know what to do next, so Thom suggested we either find your or Captain Falkner." the soldier eagerly explained.

"I'm glad you came to me, Adam. You did the right thing." Sir Almas accredited him.

"Thank you, sir." Adam humbly bowed his head.

"Let's get over there before anyone else gets hurt." Sir Almas urged motioning for the soldier to lead the way.

"Yes, sir. Right away, sir." Adam acknowledged.

He stood still and fidgeted uncertainly for a moment, before he nodded his head in the intended direction and started out across the camp the way he had come.

They picked their way through the mess of wounded, dead, weapons, and personal effects of the remains of the battle until they came to where a broken-down cart was. Beside the cart was next to a large square tent and out in front of it gathered in a half circle were a handful of soldiers, looking on with curious interest. They were gawking at whatever was at the entrance of the tent.

Thom sat on the grass several yards from the tent; holding a tore piece of tunic to a wound on his upper arm that bled profusely. Catching sight of Sir Almas and Adam, Thom gave a respectful nod and attempted to rise to his feet, but the knight waved him off.

Looking in the direction that everyone else was Sir Almas stopped short and could only stare. He was in awe and wonder at what was before him.

A wild-looking woman with raven-black snarly hair and a skin complexion as soft and dark as mahogany stood at the entrance of the tent. Her fawn eyes flashed with furious anger, as she barred her teeth and slashed her dagger defensively.

She was unlike any other woman the knight's eyes had ever beheld.

Della slashed viciously at anyone that dared to come near her and the other women in the tent, with the dagger she clutched in her hand. During all the noise and confusion of the battle; she managed to snatch the dagger off a soldier that fell dead at the entrance of the tent.

She made it her duty to protect the other women in the tent from any man that tried to come for them; and if bad came to worse, they would use the dagger to end their lives. Each woman agreed that it was better to die on their own terms than have to face being ravaged by cruel men anymore.

With the dagger, they finally had a way out.

Only it was found out that when the noise died down and there were signs that the fighting was over, that it wasn't the men of the army of Varamor that came for them. These soldiers were different; their customs were stranger, as was their language and dress. The new soldiers and knights didn't act savagely when they laid eyes on the frightened women.

Their uniforms were dark green, armor a dull grey and on the chest plate of the knights and on the banners was the image of a mighty oak tree. Many of the soldier's skin was pale, they had a gentler way about their actions. Even though most of the women couldn't understanding the words this army spoke, they understood that they were being friendly.

Instead, they were full of cautious curiosity and stood back to marvel at them with wonder.

The soldiers of the army of Oak Land wondered why any army would even think of bringing young women so close to the front lines of battle. Yet, every man knew that these poor women only served one purpose—entertainment for the enemy soldiers.

To the victorious army of Oak Land, the treatment of these poor women was most heinous and gross. They tried to approach the frightened abused women, offering kindness and freedom.

Della, though, was convinced that all men were the same. They only wanted women for brutal vicious acts and that their kindness was only a ruse. The attempts of the Oak land soldiers to get close to the women was met with strong resistance; Della ferociously slashed at any man who came near them. She was determined not to take anymore abuse.

"Sir Almas," a much-relieved soldier declared noting the presence of the knight.

"We have had a most difficult time trying to make our intentions known to them. They—they speak Varamorean, and I am not sure we can understand each other."

Sir Almas was a tall muscularly built man in his early thirties. His skin was scorched brown from the heat of the sun and his facial features were chiseled. His eyes were a soft grey, and he had lengthy dark brown hair. His demeanor was gentle as he moved with authority, his strides were slow and relaxed.

"That woman there seems to be intent on killing anyone who comes near." the soldier reported as he pointed Della out.

"They can't understand our language at all?" Sir Almas inquired taking a few steps forward before pausing.

"We don't know for sure, sir." the soldier answered.

"All right." the knight muttered thoughtfully. "I'll try my hand at it."

"Be careful, sir." Adam anxiously warned.

Before starting out again, Sir Almas unbuckled his sword belt and pulling it off, he gave the weapon to the soldier beside him. He wanted to take all precautions, just in case the young woman was able to overpower him. He didn't want her to have access to his sword.

Being wounded or killed by my own weapon would be rather embarrassing, he reflected grimly.

With a nod of acknowledgement and thanks, Sir Almas started forward with slow cautious movements. Steadily, he moved forward closing the distance between himself and the frightened cowering women. He never once took his eyes off the one that was wielding the deadly dagger. The woman was crouched low like a tiger stalking its prey.

"Easy now," he cooed softly, holding both hands out in front of him with his palms turned up. "I mean you no harm."

The woman let out a defensive grunt as she stepped towards him and slashed her blade at the knight.

"Look, we only want to help," Sir Almas reasoned pausing for a half breath.

"Grr!" she growled at him swinging at him again.

"I am not going to hurt you…I promise." The knight assured her standing still for a moment.

"Just calm down."

The woman stopped her nervous fidgeting and stared at the knight while she contemplated her next move. Sir Almas noticed her eyes darting over his protective armor, in search of a weak point.

He saw a flicker of disappointment in her eyes when she realized there was none. He watched as the young woman quickly cast a glance at the other terrified women behind her before she looked forward at him.

He felt anxiousness grip him seeing how edgy and uncertain she was. He figured that she must have felt trapped, seeing that they were surrounded by the soldiers of a new army.

Everything seemed to slow down as he watched her grip tighten around the weapon's handle before she raised the dagger toward her throat.

"NO!" Sir Almas's voice rang out.

Chapter

3

NAPPING INTO ACTION; SIR ALMAS RUSHED forward, rapidly closing the distance between himself and the woman. He reached out and grasped the wrist of the hand that held the dagger and pulled it away from her neck.

"No! No! No!" she screamed.

The knight wrestled the dagger from her grasp. As the dagger fell to the ground, Sir Almas stepped up to the angry woman and wrapped his arms around her, embracing her in a bear-hug to restrain her.

Feeling his strong arms around her, Della began to panic. She wriggled her body and kicked, fighting every inch of the way.

"Sh-shush." the knight soothed holding Della close enough that she could hardly move.

"Augh! No!" she moaned in despairing sobs.

"I can't," he insisted knowing full well what she wanted. "I won't allow it."

"Ahhh..." she bawled hanging her head.

"You're fine now. You are safe." he kept telling her.

"S...sir, what about the others?" Adam hesitantly inquired after a few moments.

"See if they will allow you to get close. If so, then find them some clean blankets and food." the knight ordered glancing over at the shaking bone-skinny women cowering in the tent.

"They must be starving."

"Yes, sir," Adam acknowledged with a curt nod and hurried off on his task.

Della insistently continued to kick and wriggle her body to try and break free from the knight's firm hold. At one point she got her arms up and began to pound against his chest in a fit of fury.

"Now, now," Sir Almas whispered in a mellow tone. "You're safe now."

"No! Never!" she countered giving a final rough bodily wiggle before she became limp in his arms.

Della was of the firm belief that the knight only had horrible intentions for her, just as other men she had seen before; his kindness was only an act.

He only wishes to take advantage of me, she told herself resignedly. *No man has taken me yet—and he won't either. Either he will die first, or I shall kill myself.*

"Are you done?" the knight questioned in a tone of annoyance as he craned his face down to look at hers.

Della didn't respond, she only huffed breathlessly from the effort of wrestling with the knight and turned her face away from his piercing gaze.

"Okay," Sir Almas announced taking a deep breath. "I am going to try and release you, but I don't want you to try anything. Got it?"

As he said this his grip on her gradually eased up.

Feeling the hold on her release; Della made her move. Launching herself upward by using his shoulder's for leverage, Della brought her feet up to his waist and gave the hardest kick she could muster. Pushing off Sir Almas she flung herself away from him toward the discarded dagger several feet away.

Sir Almas dove after the young woman. He tackled her and they both landed mere inches away from the handle of the deadly weapon.

This time he held her around the waist, face-down on the ground. She kicked and thrashed madly and began to scream in annoyance. After they wrestled for a while, Sir Almas was able to roll over with her on top of him.

He reached an arm up and took a hold of her shoulders and pinned her down on him, while holding her around the waist with his other. With his arm under her chin and so close to her mouth; Della bent her head down and sank her teeth into his exposed arm.

"Ah, ow!" the knight cried out in painful surprise.

Quickly, he pulled his arm down further and away from her mouth, laying his arm across her chest and under her arms.

Having her hands free, Della reached up and started clawing and slapping at his face.

Even suffering through the furious abuse of a bobcat; he still held onto her tightly. He was determined not to let her go—no matter what.

You won't get your way. he thought firmly as he grit his teeth against her painful blows.

The knight was impressed with how much of a seemingly untired fight the young woman was putting up. Most people would have given up a long time ago, but not this woman, in fact, she hadn't seemed to even slow down. Though, he was beginning to grow tired and irritated at the young woman's continued behavior.

He needed help with the young woman, but none of the soldiers were of any help; they all stood around gawking out of amazement and too hesitant to step in.

Moments later, the knight heard the approaching hoofbeats of a galloping horse. He was able to turn his head around enough to look over his shoulder and see who was riding up.

Relief washed over him as he saw that it was his good friend

Captain Toby Falkner. Riding up, the Captain immediately saw that Sir Almas was wrestling with a savagely wild looking young woman. Reining his mount to a quick halt, Captain Toby swung out of the saddle and hurried over to the two.

Jogging up, he reached down and managed to get a grip on both Della's wrists and with a strong heaving pull, he yanked Della off the knight. Before the woman had a chance to fully wrap her mind around what was happening; the Captain spun her in a circle, so she was facing away from him. He was able to pin her hands behind her back and held her there despite her forceful thrashing and wriggling.

"You caught yourself quite the tiger," Captain Toby remarked with a chuckle as Della continued to fight him.

"Yeah…she's far from trusting anyone of us." Sir Almas muttered as he slowly got to his feet.

"When she seemed to settle down the first time and I made the mistake of letting her go," the knight grumbled. "Right away, she gave me a kick for good measure and dove for that dagger. Either to try and kill herself again or to use it on me."

"Hmm, sounds like trouble." the Captain noted grimly.

"Perhaps," Sir Almas replied, not feeling convinced. "But could we blame her—or the others?"

"No," the Captain answered glancing over at the soldier giving aid to the other women. "No, I suppose we couldn't."

"I am going to borrow your rope." the knight said starting for the Captain's mount.

"What for?" Captain Toby asked puzzled.

"I figure that since she is bent on killing, she has to be forcibly restrained," Sir Almas said bringing the rope back over to the young woman.

"All precautions *must* be taken with this one." the Captain confirmed seriously.

"Bring her hands around to the front of her—if you can." Sir Almas requested as he made a loop.

Della fought hard against the Captain's actions, but his strength was too much for her to overcome. He held both of her wrist together while Sir Almas began to bind them.

"As much as I hate doing this, it's necessary to ensure your survival and safety. You have left me no choice."

Sir Almas wanted to convey to her, hoping she would understand his intentions.

Once he had her wrists securely tied; Sir Almas gave her about ten feet of slack line before he tied the other end of the rope to his waist.

"There, now you won't go anywhere without me," he said with a look of satisfaction.

"This rope stays on until I know for certain that you won't try to harm yourself or anyone else.

Della gave him a death-glare and clenched her fists tightly, but the look in her eyes told him that she understood.

Chapter

4

IT TOOK A HALF-DAY'S JOURNEY TO MAKE IT BACK TO THE main camp of the Oak Land army. Many of the soldiers were in the process of traveling back and forth between the two camps, collecting the spoils of war and would be for the next week or two.

When the women were settled in the camp, they were offered food and given water to wash in and given blankets to wrap themselves in. Only a small handful of soldiers were able to get near the women to lend them a hand and to comfort them, the rest of the army stood back and gave them their space.

Della, on the other hand, refused anything that was offered to her; she sat alone near a fire, making certain that she used the whole slack of the rope to keep her distance from Sir Almas. She sat with her arms crossed, glaring at anyone who passed and grunted with hatred every now and again.

"So, what are we going to do with all these women?" Captain Toby inquired crouching near the fire to stoke it.

"Once we get back to Oak Land, we can send them to the Abby and the priest can help them heal and learn to rejoin society." Sir Almas replied as he worked at removing his armor.

"We are going to try and take a half dozen frightened women; who don't know or trust us on a four-month journey back to Oak Land?" the Captain remarked raising a brow.

"What else can we do? We can't just abandon them here to fend for themselves in a stranger land or allow them to fall back into the hands of the Varamorean army." Sir Almas argued. "We wouldn't be doing them any favors."

"I'm not suggesting that we do that," Captain Toby insisted. "I am just concerned about having a couple of women with us who hate and mistrust us along for the journey."

"Do you believe they will cause trouble?" the knight asked testily.

"It's certainly possible. I know for sure that the one you have there, will cause you a lot of grief."

"Perhaps," Sir Almas said before he thoughtfully added. "I don't know, I can't really explain it…"

He paused as he looked over at the young woman.

"I guess, for some odd reason I feel responsible for her."

"She is beautiful." the Captain noted with admiration following Sir Almas's gaze.

"I don't see her that way, Toby," Sir Almas scolded knowing what his friend was suggesting. "She's only a child."

"Only a child?! She's practically a young woman for Pete's sake!"

"Hardly," Sir Almas reasoned. "She looks to be barely seventeen. Anyhow, I see her as more of a little sister and that I have to protect her."
"Ah, ever the valiant big brother," Captain Toby declared mockingly.

"Here, turn around and I'll help you get that off."

Captain Toby motioned for Sir Almas to turn his back toward him. Sir Almas did as his friend asked and the Captain worked the buckles loose before he lifted the bulky breastplate off and over the knight's head. After he set it off to the side, he gave Sir Almas a hand with his chainmail.

"Ah, that's better." Sir Almas sighed with relief as he was now down to his padded jacket, linen shirt, and riding breeches.

"It will be a relief to be home again, where wearing such heavy armor won't be necessary." Captain Falkner remarked longingly.

"You're lucky, you only have to worry about chainmail," Sir Almas pointed out as he ruffled his hair.

"Touché." the Captain agreed with a nod.

"So…how do we handle our new unique cargo?" Sir Almas put it up to the Captain.

"We will assign the group of soldiers that are giving them care now to tend the women until we reach home. We must impress upon them the need to be cautious and ever watchful of the women…they have been through so much already." Captain Toby devised in deep thought. "Handling them must be treated as a delicate process."

"Of course," Sir Almas readily agreed. "And what if we should have trouble?"

"Find the troublemakers and separate them from the main body. They will have to travel alone and under the supervision of a knight."

"Sounds good."

"What about your little friend there?" Captain Toby challenged pointing to the young woman.

"You just let me worry about her." Sir Almas assured his friend.

"She will kill you in your sleep." the Captain warned casting a suspicious glance at the young woman.

"It's just a risk I will have to take." Sir Almas countered as he gathered his armor up to set it out beside his and the Captain's tent.

"Can't be said that I didn't try to reason with you!" Captain Toby called after him.

After setting his personal effects in a neat pile; Sir Almas gazed over at the young woman, seriously contemplating the choice he had just made.

Have I gone mad? Toby is right; that woman could just as well kill me in my sleep. She is filled with hatred and mistrust; on top of it she is violently dangerous.

What am I going to do with her? He seriously mauled it over.

He had taken responsibility for her because he wanted to prevent her from harming herself. He had no idea that his decision would make her his responsibility for the remainder of the journey back to Oak Land, originally, he thought she would have gone off quietly with the rest of the women.

Oh, how wrong he had been.

Now, he was faced with the repercussions of his decision for the long haul. There was no putting her back with the rest of the group; she couldn't be allowed to be on her own. He knew that she wouldn't be long with them if she wasn't constantly watched over. Right now, she was a danger to herself more than anyone else.

As much as he hated to admit it; he couldn't leave her to fend for herself.

By the following morning the entire camp was packed up except for a small detail that was to be left behind to collect all the loot. The women were put up in a supply wagon to be taken back to the kingdom of Oak Land.

Sir Almas untied Della's rope from a tree and lashed it back around his waist. He had to tie her to a tree because he was on guard duty that night, but Captain Toby kept a close watch on the young woman. The night had passed without incident.

Della was sleeping with her back resting against the tree when Sir Almas came over and tied the rope around his waist. She was sleeping so hard that she didn't stir, until the knight pulled the rope taunt.

When she felt the slight tug, she was wide awake and alert, being startled so badly, she recoiled away from the knight. Trying to run away from the knight; the rope was pulled tight and she was abruptly yanked back to her knees.

She sat there on her knees for a moment in dumbfounded confusion.

"Ah, you won't get very far that way." the knight muttered in a patient tone.

The woman sat there with fists clenched, she glared at the knight and he could tell she was seething with anger.

"Are you hungry?" Sir Almas asked.

Della didn't reply.

"I don't know about you—but I'm famished." he said as he began walking toward the center of the camp where the cook was making food.

Della could do nothing else, but follow the knight as the rope was pulled tight. She dug her heels into the ground, making the trip over to the chow line slow.

> Her pace was so slow, that Sir Almas, usually being a patient man, was beginning to get very annoyed by her childish behavior. With his tolerance for her blatant stubbornness wearing thin, Sir Almas grasped the rope with one hand and gave it a tug now and again to force the young woman to move. These sharp little yanks got uncomfortable for Della and she eventually picked up the pace.

Standing in line for food, the knight took up two wood trays and walked along with the young woman in tow. Stopping at the biscuit basket, he held one up to the young woman for her consent. Even though she insisted on being uncooperative; the knight continued on with the practice of offering her food as they went along through the lineup.

After filling their trays with biscuits and venison stew; Sir Almas took the young woman back over to their camp spot away from the other people in the camp. He set Della's food down about five feet away from where he sat down; leaning his back against a tree he began to dig into his meal.

The young woman clenched her jaw, huffing loudly, she crossed her arms over her chest and remained standing where she had stopped.

"Suit yourself." Sir Almas said shrugging as he went on with eating.

The knight could tell by the expression on the young woman's face that she was very hungry and tempted to go for the tray of food. Yet, even facing hunger, the young woman would rather starve then take food from the knight.

"You best eat up or you'll go hungry until we stop this evening." the knight warned biting into a biscuit. "It will be a long hard day."

With reluctance, the woman slowly gave in and knelt down picking her tray up. She scooted away from the knight as far as the end of the rope. Finally sitting down, she faced the knight and kept a watchful eye on him as she began to eat.

At first, she picked at the food, but gradually she greedily scarfed it down.

Just as I thought, practically starving. Sir Almas mused with satisfaction.

Chapter

5

HEY ATE THEIR MEAL IN SILENCE FOR A TIME BEFORE the knight spoke up.

"You know, you're under my care now." He informed the woman.

"Which means I am solely responsible for you and anything you do."

Hearing this, the young woman chewed more slowly while her gaze of surprise slowly drifted up toward the knight's face.

"This means I alone will decide what shall happen to you once we reach the kingdom of Oak Land. I am in effect your benefactor."

Sir Almas set his tray aside and wiped both hands together.

"See as how you still have the brand of slavery; this may be perceived that you are my slave," Sir Almas explained. "Slavery has been outlawed in the land of Teary Isles for many years."

He paused for a moment.

"But I have a solution for this small problem, but it will involve you trusting me enough to allow me to touch your face."

At this, Della's eyes widened in fear. She dropped her tray and curled into a defensive ball, shying away from the knight.

"I promise you; I mean you no harm." he tried to assure her.

"No!" she uttered.

"Please, it will be for your own good."

"Touch me, I kill." she threatened.

"How? Your hands are bound?" the knight countered smartly.

"I wait," she spoke in broken sentences. "Right moment, I kill you."

"When you sleep."

"Oh," Sir Almas muttered nodding with conviction. "I believe you would too."

"Still, your bonds of slavery must be broken…forever. Beginning with that brand." He said pointing to the circular brand on her left temple.

"No, touch!" she objected furiously barring her teeth.

"Very well, we will keep visiting this subject daily, until you learn to see things my way." the knight remarked decidedly. "Your other friends have their slavery bands broken. You're the last one."

"No!" Della shouted at him.

"We shall see about that." Sir Almas said with a grin and nod.

"Never!" Della confirmed with a glare of hatred.

So, you believe you can outlast me for stubbornness? Sir Almas contemplated as he finished off his stew.

Just try me, woman. Stubborn ways are my greatest pastime!

Sir Almas left Della tied to his waist and put her up on a spare horse that plodded along beside him. Surprisingly, the young woman didn't try anything when the knight brought her the horse; she only calmly mounted and stayed still in the saddle waiting for Sir Almas to mount.

Della seemed uninterested in the world around them; she rode along staring down at her hands the whole time.

Odd. One would think she would be curious about the world around her. After all, she is now deep in the forest of Teary Isles, a strange new land for her. the knight pondered.

"Beautiful country, isn't it?" Sir Almas remarked glancing over at her.

Della shrugged.

"Rocks, dirt, and trees." she stated flatly.

"Oh, so you do say nice things." the knight said with a tone of sarcasm.

Della cocked her head to one side and a mischievous look spread over her face.

"Do I get a name?" Sir Almas inquired.

Della turned her attention to the forest and shook her head.

"So, you only speak when it suits you, is that it?" the knight declared thoughtfully.

They rode along in silence for a time before Sir Almas asked the question that had been nagging him all morning.

"How about that brand?"

"You touch, you die." she threatened coldly.

"All right," Sir Almas relented grumbling resignedly. "We will be making another stop within the next few hours."

"Humph." Della grunted.

Stubborn woman! Sir Almas thought irritated.

He seriously contemplated what he was going to do with her once they reached their destination. He knew right now, she trusted no one and he was probably the only person who could decently work with her.

She was so scarred from her past cruelties and mistreatments; that trust would never come easy for her. To make matters worse; she had been thrust into a strange land, into the hands of complete strangers with a different language and culture.

Learning to trust someone would be one thing, but to be forced into a new world and having to meld into a strange society could prove to be too much for her.

The knight gradually realized that he had only one option left; he had to bring her home with him.

His younger sister, Amelia lived in the house with him and the knight figured that the young woman may be more willing to readily trust his sister, than even him. With a deep contemplative thought about the matter, Sir Almas was convinced that he had it all sorted—until a thought struck him. *What would Amelia say when I bring the strange young woman home with me?*

At the creek, Sir Almas once again took the woman to a secluded spot away from the main group. Della had a drink, washed her arms and face before she sat down on the bank to rest.

"So, you're still alive." Toby remarked smartly as he approached Sir Almas.

"It appears so." the knight confirmed sitting up from his laying position. "I will stay this way, as long as I don't touch her."

"Oh, really?" Toby asked with intrigue as he sat down beside Sir Almas.

"She does speak then?"

"Yes, but only when she wants to." the knight informed.

"She has an uncommonly thick accent…even for a Varamorean."

"Truly a Forbidden Lander, eh?" Toby sighed running a hand through his reddish-blond locks.

"True to the core." Sir Almas added with an amused grin.

"She's quite a feisty one." Sir Almas said laying down on his back again.

"Have you decided what you will do with her once we get home?" the Captain pressed

"She will be staying with Amelia and me."

"Have you gone mad?!" Captain Toby burst shocked.

"She needs to be around someone she can trust—or at least feel confident around." Sir Almas reasoned patiently.

"She's been put through so much in such a short amount of time. Through so much horror that thrusting her into society on her own would be devastating."

"This woman **needs** full time care; you're a knight—with many duties, you don't have the time to babysit that woman," Captain Toby scolded.

"She is probably in such a bad way that no amount of love, care, or kindness will ever make her right."

"I suggest you find her a place where there are people equipped to deal with this sort of thing and leave her there."

"Are you telling me to abandon her?" Sir Almas asked sitting up abruptly to glare at Toby.

"You're a knight, you can't possibly care for her," the Captain reasoned motioning to the girl. "She will only be a burden to you. You need to focus on what is important in life; your career."

"You want me to give her up as a lost cause?" Sir Almas's temper began to flare.

"Almas, she will only be trouble; she has already proved that." Captain Toby tried to reason. "She will be more work than you need on your plate."

"Toby, she's not a job." Sir Almas snapped flatly. "She is a young woman who has been treated horribly and has had her trust shattered. It is not her fault that she behaves the way she does." "I will not abandon her when she needs some kind of stability in her life, right now."

"She's not your responsibility, Almas. She is like the other women; we are only helping them get to Oak Land. Then from there, they can choose where they want to go." Captain Toby said pointedly.

"She is a job. Just like the other women; getting them to safety is a mission for us to complete. After that, we leave them and go on with our lives."

"I will not just deposit her on someone else's doorstep. Being abandoned by her rescuers will be doing her no favors." Sir Almas countered firmly.

"You are making a big mistake," Captain Toby said frowning deeply.

"She will only bring you trouble and frustrations."

"Then it is my mistake to make—my burden to bear." the knight stated with conviction.

"What about Amelia," Captain Toby challenged defensively.

"What about her?"

"Aren't you being a little selfish in not thinking about her? How do you think she is going to react when you bring that—that girl home?" Captain Toby explained nodding over at the woman.

"I—" Sir Almas trailed off struggling to find the right words.

In truth, up until now, he hadn't even thought about how his sister would feel about a stranger coming to live with them.

Especially, one that was so hurt and angry at the world.

"I will cross that bridge when I come to it." he answered.

"Amelia won't take it well. You and I both know that."

"We don't know what she will think!"

"Almas," the Captain began to plead in his most reasoning tone.

"Leave it be, Toby. You will only make things worse, if you keep trying to butt in.

I am a grown man; I think I can make my own decisions and handle my own affairs." He said getting to his feet and stalked off abruptly.

"You can't say I didn't warn you!" Captain Toby called. "I care about you, Almas, and only want you to be careful with how you choose to handle this woman.

Mark my words; she is dangerous!"

Sir Almas only kept walking, he was seething with hurt and anger. He could not believe that his own good friend had turned against him about his decision to take on the care and responsibility of the young woman. He wondered why Toby was objecting to him taking in the young trouble woman.

What is so wrong with me helping that poor woman? What did she ever do so wrong?

Chapter

6

OR THE NEXT THREE WEEKS THE DIFFICULTY OF TRUST AND
mistrust went on between Sir Almas and Della. Tirelessly
and patiently, Sir Almas continued working with the young
woman; all the while he kept a careful watch on her.

The expressed many times that he was still convinced that she
was a danger to herself as well as others.

Della wondered why the knight was being kind and watched
over her. What was his plans for her were?

People are only nice and caring to you when they want something
Della thought with firm conviction.

Sir Almas sat on a log near a low fire, resting across his lap was
his long sword. He was carefully cleaning and sharpening the blade.
Della watched him with interest.

She noted how he took great care with his sword, wiping the
blade with slow steady strokes; there was a sense of almost loving

care for the weapon. Della concluded that his sword had been his closest ally in the past year or so; and this was true for most men of war.

Their weapons were a vital part of survival for them.

This caused her to reflect over the past few weeks of being the knight's ward and realized how caring and patient he was being with her. He never forced anything nor got outright angry with her. She had not received so much as a harsh word from him, even when she knew she deserved it for acting so stubborn and rude.

His words were soft, but firm. He approached her with caution and respect—something she had not known in many, many years.

What could possess a knight of all people to be the way Sir Almas was? Weren't all knights supposed to be tough, firm, uncaring people?

Why was this knight so different?

Della shivered against the cool evening breeze as it touched her exposed skin; the knight's crackling fire seem so enticing right then. Just to be near it, meant to be warmer than she felt now.

Yet, she refused to show any sign of weakness by approaching the knight's fire. She feared that the knight might be waiting for her to make such a move; then when she got close enough, he could entrap her. He could very well be waiting for an opportunity to pounce on her at any sign of her giving into his acts of kindness.

I am not the kind of fool you think I am, Sir Knight, she thought defiantly.

I didn't give in when I was with the army of Millet and I will not give in now. Nor will I fall for your pretend kindness—I have seen it all before.

Sitting so far away from the nice warm fire was torturous; the desire to be near it was almost overpowering.

"You are welcome to come share my fire." Sir Almas offered giving Della a glance as though he had read her mind.

The offer was so tempting to take up, but her instincts were telling her to stay clear of the knight and the fire—especially when he had a weapon in his hand!

Sometime later when the knight completed his task and put his sword away; he rolled his blanket out.

Della watched curiously as the knight knelt, folding his hands at his waist, bowed his head and closed his eyes. He moved his lips as though he was speaking to someone, but there came no sound, not even a whisper.

What is he doing? Della asked herself.

She watched him with puzzled wonder for the next five minutes, until he had finished and got up to stoke the fire. The knight looked over at her from across the fire and slightly grinned.

"I was praying," he explained. "I speak to my God and his son Jesus each night."

It now made sense to Della why the knight had done what he had. She had seen things like this before, but it was with loud shouting, incantations, and the cutting of one's self to appeal to the gods.

She thought it was strange that the knight believed in only one God and that this God had a son.

What a strange religion he must have? she pondered.

Della silently watched the knight as he settled down on his blanket and soon drifted off to sleep. She stayed up for the next few hours watching the knight sleep.

Slowly, sleep gradually overcame Della, until she curled into a tight ball and drifted off.

When Della woke the following morning and looked over to where the knight had been sleeping. She was surprised to see his bedroll empty. In the camp around them most people were sleeping, but there were a few soldiers walking around the camp on patrol.

Finally!

Della knew this was her one chance to make her escape. She scrambled to her feet, running over to where the knight's bedroll was. Suddenly, she saw the boots of Captain Falkner poking out of the doorway of the tent in front of her and she froze in her tracks.

Holding her breath, she waited for a few moments, but when

the Captain did not move; she figured that he must have been sound asleep. Quickly, she rummaged her way through the knight's bedroll and pack until she found the dagger he had taken from her earlier.

She sliced through the rope close to her waist. Once the rope was cut off, she jumped to her feet and tossing the dagger aside she ran off into the thickly overgrown forest.

Della felt that with no one nearby to stop her, she would be free to make a clean get away. She ran on blindly, crashing through the overgrown brush and shrubs. Low branches scratched and clawed at her face and arms; the sharp rocks were cutting her bare feet.

The forest was so dense that Della did not know what direction she was going in and every turn she took she was only faced with more trees. She could not see the sun or sky above because the canopy of branches and leaves blocked her view.

Suddenly, from behind her, she could hear the steady thundering of a horse's hoofbeats coming. Glancing behind her, Della could only see shrubbery and trees; there was nothing there.

Someone was chasing her!

Filled with panicked anxiety and desperation; Della ran faster. She moved along so fast that she could barely catch her breath and her legs were starting to feel wobbly. Tears stung the back of her eyelids, her sides heaving from the strain.

I will not go back! I...cannot!

When she leapt over a fallen tree in her path; the ground on the other side vanished beneath her feet; giving way to a dead-drop slope.

All Della got out was a strangled yelp of surprise and fear as she tumbled downward, head-over-heels.

Sir Almas had been riding back to his camping spot after scouting the area for the journey ahead. As he was riding up to his and Captain Toby's tent, he caught a glimpse of Della before she disappeared into the cover of the thick foliage.

Without hesitation, he spurred his mount onward and rode in

pursuit of the girl. He chased her through the forest for quite a way, until he came to the spot where he knew a gorge was.

Oh, no! he gasped inwardly with deep dread.

He already knew what had happened to the poor woman.

There is no way she would have seen it running scared. I nearly fell into it a few days ago myself.

Hauling on the reins of his mount; Sir Almas swung out of the saddle even before the animal came to a complete stop. When he came to the edge of the gorge; stopping before the fallen tree he looked over the edge into the deep crevasse.

He could not see to the bottom because it was too overgrown with greenery and filled with fallen trees, which made it look dark and shadowy. Pulling his sword from his scabbard; he stuck it into the tree before he climbed over the log.

Do not want to risk losing this. he told himself.

Holding onto the tree, he carefully lowered himself down the other side, entering the gorge. He kept his back to the wall of it as he slowly slid down the steep sloping ground. Several times, he almost plummeted face-first down the hillside because there were so many jagged rocks, roots and branches jutting out of the gorge wall.

Nearing what he was sure had to be the bottom, he could finally clearly see where the woman had tumbled down. There were claw-like finger marks dug into the muddy wall and broken branches from where she fell.

The knight concluded she would have suffered either one of two fates upon reaching the ground; either she would be lying on the grass knocked out cold or she would be able to get up and continue her fleeing.

His boots thudded against the solid ground of the forest floor and Sir Almas rose out of his crouching position. Straightening up, he looked around on the ground for any sign of the young woman among the bed of broken branches and dry, dead leaves.

He only saw evidence of where she had hit the ground and got back to her feet before running on again.

The chase had resumed.

Chapter

7

IT WAS APPARENT THAT THE YOUNG WOMAN HAD BEEN TOO beat up from her tumble down the hill that she was not able to get away quickly. Sir Almas could hear twigs snapping from her crashing through the trees. Looking to the southwest he could see branches wiggling from where the girl had passed through moments ago.

Now, tracking her was not going to be too difficult she was running clumsy from her injuries.

Upon reaching the bottom of the hill, Della was in a full panic. She was badly bruised and scraped up from the tumble down the hillside; her ankle had twisted severely in the fall. Despite this and the painful protest of her injured joint; Della first crawled and then stumbled to her feet before limping away at a clumsy jog.

When she managed to get her feet under her, she limped off as fast as she could toward the thick cover of the foliage.

She was desperate to escape!

In her panic, she got lost and switched direction several times, not knowing which way to turn next. Della stumbled, staggered, and wildly crashed through the thick undergrowth. Every inch of the forest looked the same as the last and she couldn't get her bearings.

Worst still, was that the trees were obstructing the sun overhead, it was impossible for her to use it as a guide to figure out what direction to go. Her legs felt like rubber after her constant running and fall down the slope, that they refused to function decently.

Della felt too exhausted to go on.

Pausing for a half-second, her eyes locked on a wide old pine tree; it looked to be a good place to hide behind. Shakily, she hurried over to the tree and made her way around it, she had it in mind to hide on the other side.

Coming around the opposite side, she came face-to-face with her pursuer.

It was the knight.

Seeing who it was, Della tried to back up, but the knight's hand shot out and he grasped her by the arm and yanked her toward him. She twisted away from him and tried to forcibly pull herself free, but her attempt was useless.

Sir Almas took two strides forward and wrapped his arms around the girl from behind: pinning her swinging arms downward at her sides. She moaned loudly in protest as she began to fight wildly, violently wiggling against his hold.

"No, no, no!" she wailed.

He lifted her feet up off the ground as she kicked and thrashed around madly in a desperate attempt to escape.

"You're not going to make it easy, are you?" he muttered through clenched teeth. "Are you?!"

Della began to groan loudly, wriggling harder and she swung her arms and legs, kicking viciously with her legs.

"Just take it easy." the knight's tone reflected how impatient he had become with her relentless behavior.

She was acting like a cornered wild cat; desperate to do anything to get free of his hold on her.

"I will not let you go, until you stop fighting me." he told her plainly.

"Never!" she screamed in defiance.

You cannot fight me forever. Sir Almas thought stubbornly.

His arms were aching from the strain of holding out against the woman's tireless struggle.

"Augh!!!" she wailed tearfully.

With a strong heaving effort, the young woman raised her knees up high and kicked her feet back as hard as possible, with lightning fast movement. The blow caught Sir Almas full in the stomach between his ribs and waist. The knight let out a muffled gasp as the breath was knocked out of him and he had to fight against the surge of intense pain rising from his battle wound.

He partly bent over but kept his hold on the woman.

The pain he felt was so strong that all his anger and frustrations boiled over. He shoved the young woman from his arms, sending her falling forward to her knees and she was caught completely unaware.

Sir Almas held a hand to his side where the woman had kicked him and took steps back putting distance between the two of them. He struggled to catch his breath trying to overcome the intense pain.

He felt at the end of his rope with the young woman's wearisome behavior.

Della rolled onto her back before she sat up in a curled position and stared up at the knight in startled surprise.

"That's it!" he grunted hoarsely.

"If you are so set on fleeing, then go!"

"I have tried so hard…so very hard, to help you. To try and make you understand that I only want to help you. To look out for your wellbeing and safety.

Yet, you refuse to listen or understand." the knight exclaimed in frustration.

Della stared up at him in utter shock, she could only sit there and wonder what his next course of action was going to be. She feared retaliation for her kicking him so brutally.

"If you don't want me to help you; then I am letting you go. I am doing neither of us any favors by keeping you against your will. It is hard on you and consumes much of my time.

Get up and go! Go on, run!" he challenged jabbing a finger in the direction she had been running toward.

"I can assure you that you will not last longer than a month out here. You are in a land that is not your own and you know no one... not that there is a single soul in these parts to be known.

Eventually, you could get recaptured by someone with devious intentions for you or in a matter of days you will die from starvation or exposure." he went on shaking his head.

"No one really knows this part of the forest; not even the Golden Arrows or Devin Bandits."

"If you are so convinced that you can survive on your own out here, then by all means be on your way. But be assured that no one will care for you out there."

There was a tone of bitter sympathy in his voice as he looked away from her. He rubbed his side where she had kicked him and looking upward, he winced in pain. Della leaned forward, her actions full of hesitant uncertainty.

"No one will care for you...not the way I do. I have tried to watch over you like I would for my own sister." the knight muttered looking away from her.

Della stayed where she was, carefully considering her next move. Gradually, she began to feel more remorse for her actions toward the knight and his patient kindness.

"I will not," the knight paused to suck in a deep breath as he straightened up. "I will not hold you against your will any longer. You're free to go...farewell."

Still holding a hand to his side, the knight winced as he took a step forward and began to limp away from the young woman. She was surprised that the knight was choosing to leave her behind. He was not going to force her to return to camp with him.

What kind of good possesses this man? How can he be so forgiving? Della wondered puzzled by the knight's attitude towards her.

She watched as he went; the kick had clearly hindered him. Not one time, did he stop or look over his shoulder at her, he was truly letting her go.

Something inside her did not want him to go.

"Y—you are hurt." she blurted out suddenly.

"Excuse me?" the knight halted at once, half-turning towards her.

"You are hurt, are you not?" she repeated slowly rising to her knees.

"Um…yes." he replied easily. "During the last battle with the Varamor army, but in a few more weeks it will be nothing more than another scar."

"Being hurt means nothing to you?" she asked with interest.

"I am a knight, it's part of the job. You just get used to the wounds and injures after a time." Sir Almas replied before he turned and started on his way again.

Della stood for a moment longer watching the knight as he moved away from her. In that moment, she made up her mind. She was going to willingly stay with the knight, at least until they got to this kingdom of Oak Land, once there she could decide what to do next.

Leaves rustled under feet and twigs snapped as she limped along after the knight. He checked his paced ever-so-slightly, but did not turn, Della knew he was aware of her following him.

Chapter

8

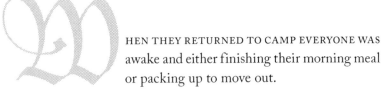 HEN THEY RETURNED TO CAMP EVERYONE WAS awake and either finishing their morning meal or packing up to move out.

"There you are!" Captain Toby declared in a tone of relief as he approached them.

"Yes, here we are." Sir Almas replied in a mock-tone.

"We were beginning to wonder what had happened to the two of you, especially when your horse came galloping back into camp some time ago without you."

"I feared that some kind of harm might have befallen you." the Captain explained as he looked from Sir Almas to the lagging young woman.

"It almost did." Sir Almas mumbled in an undertone.

"Excuse me?" Captain Toby remarked not hearing what Sir Almas had said.

"Oh, nothing," the knight countered quickly. "The young woman wanted to go on a walk through the forest and stretch her legs before we got underway again this morning."

The Captain gave a slow nod at this, but the look in his eyes made it clear that he was not convince of Sir Almas's reasoning. His gaze of suspicion never left the young woman.

"Well, you two best get packed up," Captain Toby ordered snapping into action.

"We will be on our way within the next half-hour."

"Yes, sir." Sir Almas acknowledged his superior officer with a curt nod.

The Captain lingered for a while longer giving the young woman a hard, untrusting glare before he dismissively shook his head and strode away.

Sir Almas stared after his friend; the nervous anxious feeling he had when Captain Toby confronted him was slowly dissipating. Even though the Captain was a close dear friend; he knew he outranked him in authority. If at any time, Captain Toby felt that the young woman was becoming too troublesome for Sir Almas, he could easily have her taken away and put with the rest of the girls and women.

Sir Almas knew that he was walking a very tight rope and even the slightest misstep would be noted.

If I am not careful, I could lose her, he reflected as he looked back at her.

Please be good from now on—or you'll be taken away and I will not be able to help you. If you be taken away, I may never see you again.

Sir Almas wished so badly that he could convey to the young woman how delicate their situation was. He needed her to understand that they were only on a trial basis, until they got back to the kingdom of Oak Land.

Sir Almas did not utter a word as he went over to where his horse had been retied beside the girl's horse. The knight began to make a check on the tack and tighten the girth on the saddle of the girl's horse.

To his surprise, Della put the fire out and began to roll the blankets up and tie them.

In his observation of her, he noticed that it appeared that her ankle was causing her great discomfort and that she must have injured it in the fall. After tightening the girth on her horse, he went over to his saddle bag and dug a bandage out. Cautiously, he came up behind the young woman as she was tying the last bedroll up.

Hearing his boots on the leaves behind her; the young woman spun around clumsily and fell onto her backside. Falling back, she jarred her hurt ankle and let out a pain filled yelp. Quickly and defensively, she slid back away from him; her eyes flashing in fear.

"Whoa, easy now." Sir Almas reasoned stopping short.

"It's okay. Won't hurt you."

Not convinced, the young woman continued with her retreat away from his grasp.

"Hold on, now." H e pleaded with her for understanding.

He lifted the bandage up for her to see.

"I only want to help."

The woman stopped and stared at him in wide-eyed fear.

"It looks to me like you might have badly twisted your ankle." he pointed out in his soft friendly tone.

"I only want to wrap your injured foot with this. Trust me, it will help."

With careful slow movements the knight got down on his knees close to the young woman's hurt foot.

"May I?" he asked motioning to the reddening swollen foot.

For a small moment, the woman seemed contemplate her next course of action, but she slowly moved her foot and lifted it toward Sir Almas. Gently, the knight took a hold of her ankle in one hand and felt it with his other hand.

The girl clenched her teeth and hissed against the throbbing pain that ran up her ankle. For a second, Sir Almas feared that the woman would jerk her foot away, but she just toughed out the pain.

"Good news," Sir Almas announced with relief. "It's not broken. Wrapping it with this bandage will help stabilize it so it will heal faster."

The young woman gave a slight nod of understanding and allowed him to bind her ankle.

Thank you, Lord. Sir Almas prayed in earnest.

Thank you for helping her to understand and for letting me do this. Thank you for watching over her, that she was not more seriously injured.

Maybe…just maybe he was beginning to make headway with the troubled girl.

When they finished packing, and the bedrolls were tied behind the saddles; Sir Almas led the horses over to where the young woman stood. It felt good not to have to have her tied to him anymore, and he believed that the young woman must have felt the same way about it too.

"Ready?" he asked looking over at the woman holding the reins of the horse out to her.

The young woman limped over and took the reins from the knight and moved away from his reach again. Limping up beside the horse, she stood staring at the saddle for a few moments trying to figure out how she was going to get into the saddle with her bum ankle.

"Do you mind?" Sir Almas inquired motioning to lift her into the saddle.

She looked at him with her timid eyes and nodded her consent. Sir Almas stepped up beside her and gently gathered her up in his arms and swung her onto the horse's back.

"Are you okay?" he asked with concern once she was in the saddle.

She looked down at him and only gave a casual shrug.

"All right," the knight acknowledged with a nod of approval.

He went back to his horse and swung into the saddle before he motioned for the girl to follow his lead. With Della riding closely behind him, they weaved their way carefully through the bustling camp. The knight picked their way through the camp until they were at the head of the trail and began their journey onward.

The forest was fairly warm and balmy, and the dense foliage

made a canopy overhead. Little narrow shafts of sunlight were filtering through the leaves and branches, making the trail appear magical. The air smelled sweet and fresh, especially from the warm rain two nights before.

The army of Oak Land was now just crossing into the north-western edge of the kingdom of Delmar.

Only a hundred and twelve miles until we reach home. Sir Almas told himself wistfully as he closed his eyes for a moment to picture his beloved homeland as he last remembered it.

Glancing over at the young woman, who was now riding beside him; he felt that it would be good to tell her something about her new soon-to-be home.

"We're nearly home." he remarked as he pulled even with her.

"Right now, we just entered the boarder of the kingdom of Delmar. You see Teary Isles has a wide variety of climates." He went on.

"There's the kingdom of Sand Land that is mostly hot, dry, and arid; with little to no snow in the winter months. Then there are the kingdoms of Hitterdal Land and Wades Worth; they both have similar climates of six and a half months of summer growing seasons and the winters are mild.

They do not get much snow during the winter, but their winters are icy cold and windy.

The kingdom of Ravens Burg is where the King and Queen of Teary Isles live. That kingdom has wet, moderately warm summers, but it is not an ideal place to live unless you like the rainy seasons.

Then there is the kingdom of Brooklyn Falls; that kingdom is up in the mountain ranges and it is almost cold all year around, except for short mild summers.

Last, but certainly never least, are the kingdoms of Oak Land and Delmar. For both kingdoms, the climate is very moderate, warm summers and short winters. During the winter months there is almost never snow and it is not too cold, so it is still an enjoyable season.

To me, living here is a literal paradise."

Della gazed at the knight and nodded now and again as he fondly spoke of his homeland; to her it was of little interest, but she knew it was important to the knight to tell her about the place they were headed to.

"I think you should find Oak Land is a lovely place," Sir Alma's voice took on a dreamy tone.

"There is an open market area where all manners of wares are sold and bought. Scattered all about the city are little shacks and houses; built with stone, while others are fashioned from wood and thatch.

The people are kind and friendly and the atmosphere around the castle is very hospitable."

"H—Hospitable?" Della was unfamiliar with a strange word.

"It means friendly or welcoming." The knight explained readily.

What strange customs and words these people have. Della pondered.

"Grant it; Oak Land and Delmar lie deep in the forest of Teary Isles and we don't get much for visitors. It is only during the harvest festivals do we see people from neighboring kingdoms. Though during the festival, the kingdom of Delmar isolates itself—they do not like to mingle with the people from other kingdoms, except for Oak Land.

Though, I can't tell you why." Sir Almas went on enthusiastically.

"Anyhow, we have the largest set-up for festival tournaments in all of Teary Isles and the best arena for jousting games.

Occasionally, the King of Teary Isles attends the games—paying us a great honor. King Hamish is a great man, it is a real delight to hear him speak, even just to see him is something special.

The festival lasts a total of two weeks."

Della nodded now and again in a lolling manner as the knight eagerly went on about his home kingdom. She was amazed at how the knight seemed to love his home kingdom—more than she had seen from anyone else.

Y EVENING, THE ARMY HAD COVERED OVER TWENTY miles, which wasn't bad for the amount of wounded and loot they were carrying. When the army stopped and set up for the night; Sir Almas left the young girl on her own near a clearing.

Della did not mind being left alone near the knight's tent, in fact, she felt safer that way. Being around fewer people was a good thing for her, it meant less chances of danger. While the knight was away, she set to work gathering wood to make a fire.

The knight had gone off to help the other soldiers set up camp before he and a small hunting party went off into the forest to hunt for game. They returned hours later with a large fat deer. Everyone was happy for the change in cuisine because it meant a break from continuously eating rabbit, squirrel, or bird.

The knight was able to precure a sizeable slice of meat for her,

Captain Toby, and himself. Coming back to where Della was, he rekindled the low burning fire before he placed the slab of meat on a stick to slow roast over the flames.

Della was still uncertain of what the knight's intentions were regarding her. To be safe, she stayed on the opposite side of the fire several feet away from him. Her ankle was throbbing with a dull constant pain, so that she had to seat herself on the ground to rest, with her injured leg stretched out before her.

With a gaze of guarded curiosity, Della watched the knight from where she sat as he set to work laying out their bedrolls for the night.

"We'll be having a treat tonight," the knight remarked aloud with a tone of delight.

"Roast venison. Hmmm—I can just about taste it."

Della gave only a faint smile that she kept hidden by looking down at her lap. She too shared the knight's enthusiasm for eating the succulent piece of meat.

From his crouching position near the fire, Sir Almas could not help but to take special notice of the young woman. Before, when he had to forcibly restrain the girl and they were always butting heads he never paid her appearance much mind.

That had all changed.

Only now, when he was beginning to trust her, and she was not trying to find some new way to escape; it was as though their relationship had been somehow altered.

He *really* noticed her.

Her complexion was a dark brown giving her skin a glowing appearance, even though it was smudged with dirt, bruised, and had small scrapes from her fall down the gorge. Her eyes were almond shaped and chestnut brown.

Her long raven-black hair was wavy and matted with leaves, dirt, and sticks as it hung loosely about her shoulders. She had a small slight frame, mostly due to starving for such an extended period. With proper nutrition she could put on a healthy weight and would be a most stunningly beautiful woman.

She was not very tall, a few inches shorter than his own sister; Amelia, but for what she lacked in height she made up for with her fierce personality. The young woman's face was small and elegantly shaped; there was a striking wild look about her appearance.

The skirt she wore was fashioned from leather and deer hide; barely long enough to decently cover her buttocks. The top she wore was made of beads, but her arms and chest were bare; it revealed too much at times.

The clothes were not suitable for the cooler climate they were entering. Though, the knight knew that the clothes were not intended for practical functionality, but to make her body more appealing to lonely desperate men.

Change will be difficult for her. the knight reflected with sympathy knowing that she was bound for an entirely foreign way of life.

On the side of her head beside her left eye was the wide circular brand of ownership of the slave trade. This mark was accompanied by double wide wrist bracelet brands on either wrist.

Poor woman, he sighed inwardly.

She will carry those brands with her forever.

When the meat was roasted; Sir Almas sliced a chunk off and laid it on a flat piece of bark. Cautiously, with slow steps he made his way around the other side of the fire and over to where the young woman was sitting. Instinctively, seeing him approaching her, she reacted and began to scoot away.

"Whoa, whoa." Sir Almas appealed.

Stopping short, he held his free hand up and motioned for her to stop moving away. She gave him her full attention and stopped moving backwards. Wanting to repay her willingness to do as he asked; the knight bent down and set the piece of bark on the ground.

"This is yours," he encouraged with a friendly smile and nod of his head. "Go on, eat up."

The young woman did not flinch as she stayed where she was and continued to stare at him. Sir Almas took it as his cue and slowly backed away. Only when he was back on his side of the fire did the woman move toward the meat and picked it up.

We are making progress. He told himself trying to stay positive even though inwardly he felt defeated by her continual lack of trust

Baby steps. One day…hopefully, she will come around.

Captain Toby came in for a light meal and short conversation with Sir Almas before he had to go back out on patrol duties. He tried again to reason with Sir Almas about sending the young woman with the other women once they reached home.

Yet, Sir Almas kept insisting to his friend that it would be more harmful to the woman to shove her off with the rest of the women. He pointed out how the woman was had already improved while just being around him.

She no longer had to be restrained and that she had helped them on more than one occasion. Needless to say; the Captain was not fully convinced, he believed that the young woman would only bring strife and trouble wherever she went.

Before parting company with Sir Almas, he warned his friend not to become too attached to the girl. Regardless of what the knight believed; the authority in Oak Land could still decide to take her away from him.

If that happened, then there was nothing either of them could do about it.

The Baron of Oak Land and his council was the final authority on all matters concerning the people and loot brought to the kingdom. Sir Almas hated that the young woman really had no say on her future and once again it was up to others to decide her fate. All he wanted was what was best for her and to do everything in his abilities to protect her—but when he got to Oak Land, he knew he wouldn't be able to.

"Don't get attached, Almas," the Captain warned mounting his horse.

"You don't have final say. What happens to her is not up to us."

"I know, I know." Sir Almas acknowledged feeling frustrated. "I just wish there was something more I could do."

"I want you to know something," his friend said with a sympathetic look in his eyes.

"Were it solely up to me...I would let you keep her with you, because as far as I can see, you are the best chance she has. You are good for her."

"Thanks Toby." the knight said flashing a weak smile.

It felt good to know that his friend was finally supportive of him trying to help the young woman. Though, it did not ease the anxiety that he felt regarding what kind of future awaited the young woman once they got back to Oak Land.

A good future...I hope. he thought wistfully.

Chapter

10

I T WAS LATE INTO THE NIGHT AND MOST OF THE SOLDIERS were settling down to sleep. Della was sitting alone near the Captain's tent, far from anyone else including the knight. The night air was far chillier than it had been lately, and Della was really feeling it. Her clothes proved to be little warmth or protection against the harsher elements.

She curled in a tight ball; her knees were brought up close to her chest and her arms were wrapped around her legs to keep the warmth in. The fire that had been warming her, was gradually starting to die down and she was too afraid to go off and fetch more firewood because the knight sat nearby. She watched as the knight let the flames of the fire die, while he got ready for bed.

She must be getting mighty cold sitting so far away from the fire. Sir Almas mused as he glanced in her direction.

He realized that his heavy bear-skin cloak was draped over his horse's back. He was accustomed to the weather in the territory and had no need for the cloak, but the young woman was not prepared for the temperature changes.

Getting up from his blanket, he made his way over to where their horses were tethered, untying the cloak from the saddle he made his way back over to the young woman. When he came within a few paces of her, he slowed down.

Seeing his approach, she snapped into action and began to scoot away from him again. This time, her expression was more of fear than anger, as it had been before.

"Take it easy," he advised when he came close. "It's all right. I only want to help."

The woman continued to cower away from him and backed off, until her back was pressed against a clump of bushes. Her eyes were intensely locked on him with mistrust.

"Here, use it to keep yourself warm." he suggested showing her how to use it.

Halting a few feet away, he laid the cloak on the ground before taking a few steps backward and waited.

"Go ahead."

Several minutes passed before the woman felt it was safe to move. Hesitantly, she slid forward on her good knee and thigh toward the cloak. Using her arms; she pulled herself across the ground up to the cloak.

Her eyes warily remained locked on the knight.

Reaching the cloak, she grasped the edge of it. Quickly, she yanked it toward her chest defensively. Once she had it balled up underneath one arm; she retreated toward the clump of bushes behind her. Feeling she was at a safe enough distance; she wrapped the cloak around herself tightly.

Smiling to himself; Sir Almas felt slightly triumphant at the young woman accepting the cloak from him. Turning away, the knight headed off toward the woods in search of more kindling for the fire.

It was the littlest reactions from the young woman that meant the most to the knight. It confirmed what he always believed about her. That the young woman was not beyond hope or help.

Sir Almas returned to rekindle the fire once more before he settled down on his bedroll to get a little sleep.

"There," he declared with a sigh of satisfaction.

"We should be set for the rest of the night."

Sneaking a look at the young woman he saw that she was relaxed, and her eyes held a flicker of tired curiosity.

"You should come in closer to the fire," the knight invited. "You'll stay warmer that way."

The woman stayed where she was, but her inquisitive eyes followed his every move.

"All right," he said shrugging. "Suit yourself."

The bruises, cuts, and scars from the brutality she had suffered at the hands of her masters showed on her skin. Even in the dim glow of the firelight the marks were very noticeable. Some scars would remain forever as a testament to her past life of how cruel her fellow man had been.

The knight couldn't help but feel pity for her and all the horrifically terrible events that she had to endure.

No one should ever have to endure what you have, Sir Almas reflected as he gazed mournfully upon her.

You are only a child.

Eventually, the woman ventured closer to the fire by a few feet, but watched him with a look of stark fear. Keeping his eyes trained on her; Sir Almas laid down to sleep. His gaze remained on her until he drifted off to a deep restful slumber.

Chapter

11

Upon waking up the following morning, Sir Almas was surprised to discover the young woman was sound asleep just on the opposite side of the fire. Sometime during the night, she had become brave enough to come near the fire to sleep.

Well, she is beginning to come around. the knight pondered.

Getting up as carefully and quietly as possible, so he didn't wake the young woman; Sir Almas made his way across the camp to where the cook was, to pick up something to eat for breakfast. He grabbed half a loaf of bread, jerky, and a partial jug of mead and two cups before he headed back to his camping spot.

When he returned the woman was awake and sitting up with the cloak wrapped tightly around her. She looked up at him with tired eyes before she yawned—not fully being awake yet.

"Got something for us to eat." he announced holding the provisions up.

Exercising the same respectful caution, he laid the food and water down on the ground for the woman before he stepped away. The woman crawled forward willingly, the fearful hesitancy from the night before had disappeared. Still, she regarded the knight with a suspicious gaze as she began to eat with delighted eagerness.

He knew there was a long way to go with the woman, but at least progress was being made.

Della's gaze was no longer full of resentment, but acceptance and curious wonder. Sir Almas found himself wondering what the young woman must have been thinking about. Perhaps, she was pondering why he was being so kind and caring and why he treated her so well.

Another thought had popped into his mind that had not occurred to him in several days.

The brand of slavery on the side of her head.

They were less than a two weeks' journey from the boarder of the kingdom of Oak Land. Slavery was highly illegal in the kingdom; and it was punishable by death. He had to do something about that brand—soon.

There is no time like the present. he told himself with resolve.

Taking the knife tucked in his sword belt, Sir Almas walked over to the dying fire. Placing a few more pieces of wood on the low flames and stoking it up; he stuck the tip of the knife's blade in the hot coals.

The woman was intently watching the knight's actions and seeing what he had just done, she paused from her eating. Fear shone in her eyes as she watched him, it was evident that she was afraid of what his plans were for the knife.

Several minutes passed before the knight was able to remove the red-hot knife tip from the coals. Rising slowly to his feet, he turned and began coming near the woman. She dropped the food in her hand and cowered away from the knight and the weapon in his hand.

"Hold on, easy," he soothed. "I must break the line of bondage on your face. That circular ring represents that which is very illegal here in Teary Isles.

If I do not break the ring, then you will be taken from me and I could be executed for breaking one of our most sacred laws."

The woman stopped scooting away from him when he told her this. She was uneasy about him coming so close to her but understood what his intentions for her were.

"This will sting and hurt for some time, I am sorry about this." he apologized as he knelt beside her.

Gingerly, she allowed him to cradle her chin in the palm of his hand and put the tip of the knife blade against her temple. There was a sizzling sound as the blade touched her skin and the smell of burnt flesh filled the air.

The woman clenched her teeth, winced, and moaned against the stinging pain. Her eyes were intensely locked on the knight's, but she refused to cry out—no matter how much it hurt.

"There…all done." He announced pulling the blade away as he let her chin slide out of his palm.

When he was finished the young woman rapidly crawled away from him and when she was a safe distance away; she tenderly touched her fingers to the fresh line that ran through the brand on the side of her temple.

Now a wide line ran through one side of the ring: a mark of freedom.

Much to Sir Almas' surprise she never cried out nor shed a single tear through the entire process.

She is a strong woman, Sir Almas approved proudly.

A strong woman indeed.

"We'll be setting out again soon—so you better get ready." he warned before heading off to find Captain Toby and discuss the plan of action for the day.

In the following days, Della began to warm to Sir Almas. Of all the men in the army of Oak Land he was the only one she felt that she could feel safe around. She could not trust him, but she also knew that he wouldn't try to hurt her—or that's what she wanted to believe.

Instead, of staying far away from him, she shared his fire and did not treat him with angry glares or withdraw away with mistrust. She may not have trusted him, but she knew she did not fear him anymore.

The country of Oak Land was every bit as beautiful and sweeping as the knight had told her.

The main city and great house stood in a clearing with the forest of Teary Isles surrounding it. From the edges of the city wall were a multitude of fields, some were planted with wheat, while others had potatoes and an assortment of vegetables, and herbs. Off the main highway was another well-worn path that was set between the fields and led back into the forest.

Men and women in simple clothes of peasantry went back and forth on their daily rituals. Just outside the main gate were a few quick-setup booths where merchants were selling their wares, such as weaponry, clothing, cooking utensils, and foods.

Guarding the main gate were four Oak Land soldiers, these men only wore dark green uniforms with the same embroidered image of an oak tree on their tunics and carried long spears.

Within the gates was the main city, the houses were built mainly of wood and stone with thatch roofs, except for the wealthier housing which were fashioned from mortar and were twice the size of the poor peasant's house.

The Great House where the Baron and his family lived was made from large red-black timbers and the roof was white pine. The Great House was divided into three sections, one section was for the noble family, the middle section housed the great hall, feasting hall, and dance floor. The third section was to accommodate guests, some rooms were used by the tutors for the children and some rooms were to be used as a storage area.

On the peak of the two sections of the Great House, flanking the middle were small green banners with the words: **Oak Land,** stitched in bold black lettering. Over the entrance of the middle section was a large flag. This flag was dark green with the image of a mighty oak tree in the center of it, above and below the tree was the same lettering: **Oak Land.**

It was not the most elaborate Great House that Della had ever laid eyes on, but by far, it had been the most beautiful.

The people of the kingdom were a mixed multitude, Della saw villagers who resembled her people with their dark toned skin, long narrow faces, and shorter build. She even saw a few of the commoners that bore the broken bands of slavery.

There was a noticeable distinction between the two classes of people; the wealthier wore brightly colored clothes, their hair was neatly kempt, and their actions and words were more refined.

The poorer commoners wore pastel dyed clothes, made from wool and old flour sacks. The younger commoners ran about barefooted, while the adults were the only ones with footwear. Their expressions were weary and lined with years of arduous work, age, and stress. The commoners spoke with slang and in broken sentences.

Della observed that despite their disadvantages, the poorer folks seemed happier and more friendly in their actions.

When the army entered the main gates of Oak Land; nearly all the villagers came out to meet them. In a matter of moments, overjoyed women, children, and men swamped them. The army was showered lovingly with hugs and kisses, and flowers from the small children.

Guessing what was coming, Sir Almas edged his mount in closer to the young woman's. Being surrounded by so many clamoring people was overwhelming and frightening for the poor young woman.

"Stay close to me." he called to her over all the shouting and cheers.

"We will be through this soon." he tried to assure her in a steady tone.

Pale-faced, the woman shook with fear as she huddled down close to her mounts neck. The knight saw that she was deathly afraid of being torn off her mount; she clung to its mane with a death-grip.

Villagers excitedly surrounded them with wreaths, gifts, and flowers. Many of them were wives, children, parents, and friends of the returning soldiers, all overjoyed at being reunited.

"Toby!" Sir Almas shouted over to the Captain.

"Yes?" the Captain strained to see the knight through the swelling crowd that was pushing them further apart.

"I must go home for a time; I have to get her out of here." Sir Almas pointed to the young woman beside him.

"This is all too much! I will report to the barracks as soon as I get the chance."

"Almas, do you think that is wise?" his friend asked anxiously.

"I have to, Toby. She cannot handle all of this. She needs to be somewhere alone—away from all these people." he said giving the Captain a pleading look.

"She needs a home, Toby. She needs to feel safe."

"Very well," the Captain relented shaking his head with regret. "Do what you must, but report to the barracks within an hour or I will have to send someone out after you."

"Yes, Sir!" Sir Almas acknowledged with a curt salute before he took ahold of the reins of the young woman's horse and began to weave their way out of the crowd towards a side street.

Chapter

12

ELLA WAS PETRIFIED AND UNABLE TO MOVE, BUT SHE allowed the knight to lead her mount through the massing crowd closing in around her. She had never seen a reaction like this out of a kingdom's people on the return of the army.

In the kingdom of Millet, the people never celebrated the return of their army from a campaign; not even when the royal family came through the kingdom. For her people, war was a way of life; it was normal.

After several long minutes of weaving, bumping, and pushing their way through the crowding streets they emerged onto a side street. They entered down the quiet street in a sleepy area of the city. Lining either side were small clean houses made of stone or wood with thatched roofs.

A few thin villagers and children roamed about the side streets.

The older people kept their heads low and moved along slowly, the children laughed and played with each other, ignoring the newcomers.

Della noticed that these people were not rushing out to meet the returning army; they looked upset and glared with bitterness at those they passed. Most of all, she noted that they despised anyone in a uniform.

"Many of these poor people have felt the full effect of the campaign against Varamor's army," the knight described as they went along. "When the kingdom was gathering the army to wage war against Varamor most of the recruits were pulled from the poorer districts…many never came home again."

Della nodded numbly knowing all too well how the cost of war weighed heavily on the poor. In Millet, war was a common occurrence and mothers feared for the lives of their children, both boys and girls.

War had made her people bitter and hopeless.

They went along until they reached a stone house all on its own with a medium front yard area and a flat roof. The house was double the size of the rest of the homes in the area.

"This is home." the knight announced with satisfaction halting his horse a few yards away from the front of the house.

Della marveled at how white and clean the stone of the house was; out front was a little garden with tulips and roses in full bloom.

"Here, I'll help you." Sir Almas offered as he swung down from his saddle and took ahold of her mount so Della could climb down.

Della slid down; landing easily on the ground before she quickly moved back out of the reach of the knight.

"Still don't trust me?" Sir Almas remarked sounding amused as he shook his head turning to his horse.

Untying their packs and bedrolls, he led the way to the front door a nodded for the young woman to follow.

"Come along." He invited.

Carefully, juggling the heavy loads of the personal goods, Sir Almas managed to open the pine door. The house had a warm, welcoming feel to it.

It was simply furnished with only a wall tapestry on the otherwise bare west wall of the main sitting room. The tapestry was the image of an angel seated on the bank of a river pouring a vase of white water into the river.

In the center of the room was a lounge couch and an armchair beside it. Along the adjacent wall were a few shelves lined with scrolls, trinkets, and statues. Just south of the main room was a small cooking area; it had a kiln built into the wall and a small wash tub beside it. Beside the wash tub was a counter and beneath the counter was a cupboard for dishes and food goods.

On the north side of the main room were two rooms next to each other with the same heavy dark wood door, Della assumed that these must have been the bedrooms.

The house wasn't lavishly filled like the house of most of the higher society would be, but it was more than Della had ever seen.

"Go ahead." Sir Almas encouraged willingly as he set their things on the floor beside the front door.

"Make yourself at home."

"What is mine and my sister's is yours as well,"

The young woman could only stand at the threshold, her mouth agape staring at everything around her, taking it all in with awe.

Sir Almas lingered for a moment longer watching the look of awe and surprise on the young woman's face as her eyes danced over the room before them. He reckoned it was not at all what she had been expecting.

He crossed over to one of the closed bedrooms and opened the door before he disappeared inside and emerged moments later.

"You can sleep in my room for now, until some other arrangements can be made," he informed her earnestly.

"I will sleep on the couch out here for the time being."

The young woman faced him and nodded solemnly.

"Come here, I will show you around."

With uncertain cautious steps, Della silently followed the knight over to his room.

"I know it's not much, but at least you will have a nice bed to sleep on and clean clothes to wear." Sir Almas said cheerfully.

She probably has never had a bed to sleep on, you fool! he scolded himself knowing how ridiculous he must have sounded to her.

The room was large, but relatively empty. A bed sat in the center of the room against the rear wall, a bear skin blanket was draped over the maroon linen sheets and off-white pillow. Along one wall was a shelf that had a few trinkets, parchments, and miscellaneous items. Underneath the shelf was a wooden stand for armor, but the stand stood empty.

At the end of the bed was a heavy oaken chest, a wardrobe stood against the wall on the other side of the bed. Next to the wardrobe was a clay wash basin and a vase on the stand.

"Once we get you settled in; I or Amelia can take you to the market to pick up some new dresses and shoes." he explained looking down at her dirty, bruised bare feet.

Assuming the council allows you to keep her in your care. a nagging voice in the back of his mind reminded him.

He shook the thought from his mind; determined to stay hopeful and focus on helping the young woman feel welcomed in such a strange place.

"I am certain Amelia will have some old clothes you can borrow for now."

"Oh, and don't mind all this junk in the corner," he said motioning to the corner behind the door, apologetically.

"I store a few things here, because if I store it at the barracks, I risk it getting stolen."

Della nodded as she marveled at the polished silver armor, padded jacket, and greyish white tunic. She knew it was most certainly a suit of armor belonging to the legendary order of the Silver Sword knights.

She only knew of their existence from the soldiers in the camp of Millet's army that she was being held captive in. The soldiers spoke of these knights out of fear; the Silver Swords knights were an elite fighting force formed by the King of Teary Isles to protect the boarder of his country.

They were excellent warriors known for their fighting prowess as well as being honorable and trustworthy.

Could Sir Almas be one of them? she wondered as she looked up at the knight.

"Well, what do you think?" he asked curiously.

Della only bowed her head in response to show she was pleased and even began to feel herself relax. Being in the house away from the noise and crowded city made her feel safer.

She still found it difficult to trust or feel comfortable around a man like Sir Almas who was being so kind and caring.

"My sister should be home soon." Sir Almas announced after an anxious stretch of silence.

Moments later, the front door was flung open and a young fair looking young woman came hurrying in.

"Almas! Almas your home!" she cried out with breathless excitement as she rushed over toward the bedroom.

Chapter

13

OVERCOME WITH EXCITED ANTICIPATION, SIR Almas turned and hurried out of the room to greet his sister. Forgetting about the young woman for a moment he ran to his sister; having not seen her in two years.

They flew into each other's arms embracing in a tearful reunion.

"Oh, Almas," she gasped sobbing against her brother's chest.

"I prayed every day for your safe return. Tell me, are you well?"

"Quite well, certainly now that I am at home with you." he said gazing down into his sister's eyes.

"I cannot truly express how happy I am to be back home again."

"I can only imagine." Amelia said holding her brother at arm's length and looked him over, "You've lost weight. Didn't they feed you?"

"Yes, but it was nothing compared to your delicious cooking. Your food will put meat on the bones, the food we ate was barely enough to keep us going."

"Well, I will just have to remedy that, won't I?" Amelia asked blissfully. "My, it's so good to have you home again, brother."

Amelia stopped short and her smile faltered when she looked over and saw the young woman standing in the doorway of her brother's doorway. A look of uncomfortable questioning came over her face.

"Almas, who is she?" Amelia began to assume the worst, thinking her brother may have brought home a foreign wench.

"Oh, right!" he declared moving away from his sister toward the young woman. "Amelia, I would like you to me this young woman. During our last battle when we ran the enemy from their base camp, we came across a group of slave women.

Taking pity on them, we brought them home with us with plans to leave them with the Priest so he could work on rehabilitating them and helping them to eventually rejoin society. Only did I come to discover that this young woman was different from the rest; she was badly abused and defensive. She has come to a point of being comfortable to be around only me, so I brought her here." He explained eagerly as he stopped a pace away from Della and motioned towards her.

"*Almas—*"

"Look, I know what you are going to say, but you must understand, sending her off with the rest of the other women would be an act of cruelty." Sir Almas reasoned.

"Let me guess, you think you can help her?" his sister said wary and skeptical.

"Yes, I believe that we are the only ones who can help her adjust to a new living arrangement and get her to eventually learn to trust people again."

"She doesn't trust anyone?"

"Um…no, not yet." Sir Almas answered lowering his head. "She had been put through such horrors and hardships, that it will take a long time before she may ever trust anyone again."

"I don't know about this," his sister began to object.

"She's a strange woman from another country—if she has been

put though as much as you insinuate…we may not be able to help her, ever."

Sir Almas sighed and rubbed his forehead in frustration before he looked over at the young woman, her timid eyes were locked on him.

"Besides that, what about the council? What did they have to say?" his sister proposed.

He didn't immediately reply but continued to look at the young woman.

"Almas, you have told the council, haven't you?" Amelia asked impatiently.

"No," he mumbled shaking his head before looking back to his sister. "No, I have not. I had to come here right away to get her away from the crowd. She doesn't like to be around too many people; it frightens her too much."

"When are you going to tell the council? Almas, we could get in trouble for this!"

"Don't you think I know that?!" he snapped. "I told Toby that I would report to the barracks as soon as I got her settled here. Once I report in, I will bring the matter of her staying with us before the council."

"And if they say no? Will you be able to let her go?" his sister demanded knowing her brother all too well.

"Yes," he replied all too quickly.

"Almas." Amelia said in a firm undertone.

"I will have to be," Sir Almas relented glumly. "Don't worry, Toby and I have gone over this matter several times. I got into this knowing full well that her fate is not up to me. So, don't think I haven't thought it through, I have Amelia…I have."

Her brother's shoulders sagged as he faced away from her and looked off toward the world outside through the ajar front door.

She knew by her brother's behavior that he was fully committed to the cause of helping the foreign young woman out. He had allowed himself to become attached to her, knowing full well that the council could decide to send her off with the other women and there was nothing he could do to change it.

Amelia knew that her older brother was conflicted between following the laws of the kingdom or doing what he felt was the right thing to do. That was to help the young woman.

"Whatever happens, Almas, I want you to know that I am behind you all the way," his sister promised him as she walked over and laid a hand of comfort on his shoulder.

"I really hope things work out the way you want."

Sir Almas closed his eyes and let out a deep resigned breath.

14

SIR ALMAS AND HIS SISTER CONVERSED FOR A FEW
more minutes before he had to go and report to the
barracks. He explained to the young woman that he
had to leave her with his sister, and she could be trusted. Della nodded
her understanding, even though she felt fearful and awkward about
being left alone in a strange place; with a person she did not know.

So far, though, the knight hadn't done anything to harm her
or put her in danger and she figured that she didn't have to start to
worry about the intentions of the knight now.

"This all must be so overwhelming for you," Amelia noted as
she was rummaging through her wardrobe. "Just to think about it; a
strange kingdom, people, custom…and probably language. I suppose
it's a lot to take in."

Della did not know how to react to Amelia rambling on; she
stood silently beside the woman's bed, listening.

Amelia's room was the same size as her brother's; her blanket was white linen over blue sheets and a pillow. Della guessed that the knight's sister was a painter because her walls were covered with artwork. The majority of paintings were of nature scenes, such as birds, trees, mountains, and rivers.

"Here we are," Amelia declared after a moment. "These two should do for now. They are too small for me, they're not perfect, but they look well."

Saying this, she emerged from leaning into the wardrobe and turned to Della holding the two dresses draped over either arm. Both were floor length, long sleeve dresses with plain designs. One dress was a yellowish, brown striped dress with a lace up back. The other was a faded pale blue with a clasp front that went from the waistline to just below the start of the neck.

"Here's a pair of shoes to match." Amelia said holding up a pair of dark green flat shoes.

Accepting the shoes timidly, Della bowed her head in thanks. Amelia seemed awkward in the presence of the young woman, Della knew it must have been difficult for the other woman because Della never spoke.

Giving a tight smile, Amelia dipped her head in acknowledgment.

Della was in awe over the beautiful dresses and shoes; she had not had anything so fine since before her parents died.

"You can use my hair comb, ribbons, pins, and clips until we get a chance to buy you some new ones, okay?" she inquired.

Della was so overwhelmed by everything going on around her that she could only nod numbly, holding the new belongings close.

"Come on, you should put one of these on." Amelia urged with girlish glee.

Instinctively, Amelia reached out to grasp Della by her arm to lead her over to her brother's room so she could change, just as she would have done with one of her friends. Reacting defensively, Della spun away from her grasp and backed up. Taken aback, Amelia stopped short, her cheeks went flush with embarrassment and she let out a gasp realizing what she had done.

"Oh, I am so sorry," she apologized. "I forgot myself for a moment." Amelia could clearly see that the young woman was fearful of her and was slightly trembling.

"Sorry, I did not mean to frighten you," Amelia reasoned gently. "Here, why don't you follow me over to my brother's room."

Biting her bottom lip anxiously, Amelia composed herself and walked toward the knight's room. Della followed behind her, but at a distance, fearful that the knight's sister might lunge at her again.

"Which dress do you want to wear first?" Amelia asked staying by the door as the young woman walked over to the knight's bed.

Della hesitated at first, then she gave it deeper thought before she lifted the yellow and brown dress up for Amelia.

"Perfect!" Amelia approved taking the dress, seeming to have moved beyond the awkward moment of embarrassment of earlier.

"This color is going to really set off the color of your skin."

Della set the blue dress down on the bed along with the shoes.

"Here, I let you change and when you're ready I will give you a hand with the back, got it?" Amelia asked holding the dress out for the young woman again.

Taking the dress from Amelia, Della gave a curt nod of understanding.

"Good," Amelia approved as she turned and left the room.

It was not until late in the evening when Sir Almas finally returned home from his duties. After five and a half hours going over mission reports and attending meetings with the council of Oak Land; Sir Almas was exhausted.

He was happy, though, because he would be going home to his sister and he could catch up on the latest details and happenings of the kingdom since he was away. He could not wait to get home and have a delightful home cooked meal and be able to sleep in his own house.

Sleeping on the hard, lumpy ground for over two years had not been ideal. He spent many nights on the hard, cold ground or waking up to soaking rainstorms and wishing he were back home with a roof over his head.

Sir Almas loved being back home in Oak Land, he did not realize how much he missed it. The sights, sounds, and smells of the city brought back such a sentimental feeling and he decided that he would not want to part with his beloved home kingdom again.

When he reached the front door, he could already smell the delicious aroma of roast venison wafting through the door. Sighing deeply with anticipation and satisfaction as he opened the door and stepped into the house.

The small dining table was laden with the good silverware and fine crystal glasses and dishes from Keeper's Cave. These belonged to their parents and only brought out on special occasions. Sir Almas' supposed him returning home was one such special occasion.

"Well, father was the Baron of this kingdom a number of years ago. His name was Undel and mother's name was Marcie. Unfortunately, mother perished in the first attack by Sand Land during the Keltar Nor Wars.

Father ensured that Oak Land was victorious against Sand Land…but it came at the cost of his life," Amelia was explaining to the young woman as they stood near the kiln.

"Since then, brother has cared for me and our family was passed over as the ruling family of Oak Land, but Almas was granted a commission as a knight."

Della nodded now and again as Amelia continued telling her the tale of the family history.

Sir Almas kept as soundless as possible slipping his boots off at the door before taking his sword and scabbard off. He laid them on the bench near the door and snuck off to his room to wash and change.

He dressed in his loose grey linen shirt, black breeches, and heavy wool socks. When he came back into the room Amelia and the young woman were setting the food on the table. They had dishes of roast venison, mashed potatoes, and vegetables.

"Almas! I didn't hear you come in." Amelia declared when she caught sight of him.

His gaze settled upon the young woman next to his sister at once, and he flashed a pleasant smile.

She was breath-takingly beautiful. The gown set off her complexion richly and her black hair hung loosely about her shoulders in waves. It seemed strange to see her dressed like his people when he had gotten used to her dressing like a Varamorean. She did not smile back at the knight, but cast her eyes to the floor shyly.

Sir Almas found that he could not tear his eyes away from her beauty and he found himself entirely mesmerized by her.

"Earth to Almas," his sister giggled waving a hand in the air to get his attention. "Are you okay?"

Oh, y—yes," Sir Almas stammered clearing his throat as he focused on Amelia. "Shall we?"

He started forward and pulled two chairs out for his sister and the young woman at the table. Once they were both seated, he pushed their chairs forward to the table before he went around and took his own.

"This all looks and smells delicious, Amelia." He commented marveling at the array of food before them.

"Almas, do you want to say the blessing?" Amelia asked grasping his hand.

When Amelia reached for the young woman's hand, she drew it away suddenly and regarded Amelia with a wary look.

"It's okay, I won't hurt you," Amelia appealed gently. "I promise."

Still, the young woman refused to take her hand and put her hands in her lap.

"It's all right," Sir Almas sighed with a gentle smile. "Don't worry about it."

"Heavenly Father," he began as he bowed his head.

"We thank-you for this bountiful meal, for the reuniting of our family and bringing a new friend into our household. Bless us on this night and prepare us for the day to come.

In Jesus' name, Amen."

Shortly, after the prayer concluded the food was passed around, dished out and the warm joyous meal was shared.

"Well, what did the council say?" Amelia asked after they talked in length about the local happenings.

"About what?" Sir Almas asked distractedly as he stirred his potatoes.

"About the girl,"

"Huh?" the knight's head came up and he look at his sister blank faced.

"*Almas*," Amelia groaned in frustration. "What is the council's decision? Can the girl stay here or not?"

"Oh, that." the knight acknowledged dolefully.

"What's with the tone?" his sister challenged. "Was their decision not good?"

"No, it's not that." He replied shaking his head.

The knight frowned deeply, staring at his plate he fell silent.

"Almas, would you quit being despondent!" his sister snapped peevishly.

Amelia's expression softened and she regarded her brother with sympathy.

"Why are you avoiding my inquiries? Where is your mind at, brother dear?"

"I am sorry," he apologized giving his sister a faint smile. "I am just worn out, I guess. It was quite exhausting today."

"Well, maybe you best turn in an get some rest right after you finish supper." His sister advised with authority. "We can talk more tomorrow evening…when you're feeling more up to it."

"Uh-huh," her brother agreed numbly nodding, his eyes felt like they were being weighed down by sand.

"I better."

"Don't worry about the cleanup," Amelia assured looking to the young woman who ate quickly. "I am sure she and I have got everything handled, don't we?"

The young woman stopped with a piece of venison on her fork halfway to her mouth and gave a firm nod.

Sir Almas looked pleased as he smiled at the young woman's response.

"Oh, about the council," he noted his mind finally catching up with his sister's earlier questions.

"They haven't made their decision regarding her." he pointed toward the young woman.

"So, when will you know?" came Amelia's eager inquiry.

"In a few days or weeks." The knight said, disappointed. "They have too many other concerns to worry about."

"In the meantime?"

"In the meantime, she will stay with us, I suppose." Sir Almas replied shrugging. "They never indicated whether or not she had to go elsewhere. I figured that she is better off staying with us and if the council passes their ruling and she has to leave…"

Sir Almas paused not wanting to even think about the young woman leaving them.

"We will deal with that when we come to it."

"I see," his sister acknowledged with a nod. "Well, we will make the most of the time we have until we hear from the council."

"I was thinking the same thing." Her brother agreed happily. "So, tell me how the wedding plans are going?"

"I have to tell you all about the mix-up on the flowers and the building arrangements." His sister giggled shaking her head.

Sir Almas gave his full attention as his sister launched into her tales of wedding bliss and planning for the big day.

Chapter
15

With the following morning, Sir Almas was up before dawn, after having a light breakfast he headed off to duty for the day. When he left the house, his sister was just starting to get up.

Before leaving the house, he snuck over to his bedroom, cracking the door open he peaked in on the young woman and saw that she was snugly tucked under the blankets, sound asleep.

When she slept it was the only time, she looked relaxed. Sir Almas it was sad, he wondered if the young woman would ever find a way to be happy and at peace. He knew she had been put through so much in her short life and he feared the damage could be unfixable.

He truly hoped for his sister's sake that the young woman would be good for her.

Walking out onto the cobblestone street, Sir Almas sucked in a deep breath of the cool fresh morning air. It felt so good to be back home again. After being away for two years, Sir Almas could care less if he ever traveled anywhere else in the country again.

It was a short walk across the village to the castle courtyard where the training yards were. In the wee hours of the morning the city was silent and sleeping.

The only exception were the knights schooling squires and pages through archery, horsemanship, and combat tactics in the main courtyard. While other soldiers and Sword-for-Hire's sat around in groups; cleaning armor, sharpening weapons, and exchanging small talk.

The men sitting in these groups were those who had just returned from their long two-year campaign. Each man was given three day's furlough to go home, get settled in and have a rest. Some returned to love ones who missed them, while others less fortunate came home to empty houses, or their wives and lovers who found someone to replace them.

Not all the homecomings were happy.

Sir Almas had seen the aftermath of the lives of many soldiers who had given their time in service to their kingdom. Their families and loved ones were less appreciative of their sacrifice…in a way these men came home to nothing and turned out of their houses.

Sir Almas was more than grateful he did not have to count himself as one among these men; his sister was very patient and understanding. They both learned early on that they only had each other to cling to in this cruel world, but he knew this was not to last.

His sister was set to marry Captain Toby Falkner that fall after the festival and that would mean she would no longer be waiting to welcome him home and he would be on his own.

Unless I am fortunate enough to keep the young woman in my care, then we will both have something to look forward to. he reflected thoughtfully.

For him and Captain Falkner they were not given furlough time. They were put in charge of keeping the records straight and dividing the loot up among the many different areas of financial need of the kingdom. It was a long arduous process, but they were given the utmost special trust to make sure every ounce of the loot was accounted for and went to the correct places.

Sir Almas came into the back entry of the treasury storehouse of the castle. Captain Toby was already there sitting behind the oaken table with a stack of parchment pages, a quill, and ink well before him. Off to one side was a high stack of parchments that listed the various kinds of loot they collected from the enemy camp.

The two men had to go through the stack of lists and organize them into the official record scrolls.

"Ah! Almas, you finally decided to join me?" the Captain declared relief was clear on his face, when the knight came through the door.

"Well, not everyone gets up before the sun rises." the knight replied with a tone of amused sarcasm as he left his sword at the door.

"You should try it; it makes one feel refreshed." the Captain noted as he leaned back in his chair.

He had his feet up on the edge of the table, with a quill in one hand and a goblet of ale in the other hand.

"I think I will pass," Sir Almas chuckled pulling his cloak off and tossed it over the back of his chair. "What a fantastic opportunity we have been bestowed."

"I wonder how we got saddled with this detail in the first place?" Captain Toby mused.

"We are willing, hardworking men that were seen as such perfect candidates." Sir Almas replied smartly.

"Or we were foolish enough to be still hanging around when the smart ones took off as soon as they reached home?" the Captain jested.

"Hmm," the knight nodded raising a brow.

"I know one thing for certain."

"What's that?" the knight asked.

"Can't wait until two months from now when I can take leave time to get married." the Captain declared smiling wide with delight.

"Are you planning on taking the three-week furlough?"

"Absolutely, I would be a fool not to." Captain Toby replied. "My fiancée would probably kill me if I didn't."

"You mean my sister?" Sir Almas joshed. "Oh, yes, she would not be happy if you just married her and went straight back on duty."

"Of course, that, and she wouldn't be marrying me if she thought I was a fool."

"You mean, you are lucky that I gave my blessing for you to marry her."

"In all honesty," Captain Toby remarked giving the knight a mischievous look. "I would have run off with her and married her— if you didn't give your blessing. Face it, I would be a dupe not to snatch up such a smart beautiful woman as your sister."

"And I would have pursued you to the ends of the earth if I had to. She's my baby sister and I will do what I must to protect her." Sir Almas warned jokingly.

"Too true," the Captain agreed tipping his glass to his friend.

Sir Almas slid down in the chair next to the Captain and pulled a piece of parchment paper from the stack of loot listing and he set to work reading it over. While reading it he grabbed a clean scroll and quill and began to take stock.

"This is kinda redundant," he mumbled not looking up. "Onions, forks, buckles, plates…etc."

"It's all loot and therefore must be accounted for." his friend reminded him as he mimicked Marshall Dupo Jutla. "Accuracy of a kingdoms records is the key to its long-lasting success."

"Ha, sure," the knight scoffed disgruntled. "Then why isn't the Marshall down here helping us?"

"He's too important for such a menial task," Captain Toby declared dramatically. "And…he's also too smart."

"Then what does that say about us?"

Captain Toby looked at him from the corner of his eye and gave a chuckle.

"By the way, how are things going with your guest?" the Captain asked after a stretch of silence.

"Well…it's been a little rough." Sir Almas confessed.

"She hasn't changed much since the journey home and she still doesn't really speak. I think it is been most difficult on Amelia. She's trying to be patient and understanding, but I can see the strain it is putting on her."

"I'll bet it is," Captain Toby agreed understandingly. "She's a very social bubbly woman. She loves to converse with people and when they don't carry a conversation, she gets quite frustrated and fed up."

"I know, but I feel like someone like my sister can help her learn to trust again. Perhaps she may even be able to get the girl to speak again." Sir Almas spoke hopefully.

"I'm not sure about that." Captain Toby commented. "She hates, and I emphasize *hates* everyone she encounters. She has built up so much anger and mistrust, I don't think you or anyone else can help her change."

"I disagree. She does not hate everyone, in fact, she is comfortable with being around me. Besides that, she never spoke during the first few weeks of our journey home, but four weeks later she spoke. That's a change Toby, it's not nothing."

"Oh, really?" the Captain asked sarcastically as he raise a brow. "If I recall correctly, you told me the only words she uttered were threats against you."

"Yes, but it's better than nothing. At least, I found out that she wasn't a mute," Sir Almas defended. "And that she spoke as well as understands our language."

"Fine, but even if she speaks it will probably only be enough to get her by."

"I refuse to believe that she is stuck like that. Somewhere beneath all those layers of denial, mistrust, and hatred is a beautiful, intelligent, friendly young woman."

"Almas, you're not—"

"No, Toby, I am not falling in love with her. I only want to help her rediscover who she used to be. I want her to learn to enjoy the world around her. I want her to dream like the rest of us, to learn to trust again."

"I hope you're not or you may be sorely heartbroken if things don't go the way you hope. Whether you can help her or not is one thing, but if the council decides to send her away, is another entirely."

"I would be disappointed either way. I feel so bad for her; wondering why she had to endure so much abuse and hatred." Sir Almas muttered clenching his fists in anger.

"It's the way of the world," the Captain reasoned. "The way Varamor is. To them most of their people are slaves, commodities that can make them coin. They are equals to livestock and it appears that this girl was a product of the worst of that country."

"The injustice of that country is sickening to me." the knight reflected wrinkling his nose with distaste. "While we are satisfied with going to war against each other over foolish things such as trading rights and land. People are enslaved and used in the worse ways imaginable in Varamor.

If we want to go to war, we should go against Varamor and put an end to that horrid way of life once and for all. No one deserves to be a slave…ever!"

"Easy now, cool down, Almas." Captain Toby soothed. "It is what it is. Getting into war with another country isn't the right thing either. You and I both know that."

"I know, but it makes me so mad. Having that young woman around me makes me realize how messed up things are in her country."

"Don't overextend yourself, Almas, or you'll only end up getting hurt." his friend warned as he started listing things off on his scroll.

"I know what I am doing, so stop worrying about me and the young woman." Sir Almas assured him as he began to tend to his work.

Captain Toby fell silent and went back to work.

What will I do if I am unable to help her?

Am I willing to let her go if the council decides she must go to the Priest's shelter home?

Sir Almas sighed inwardly, feeling dejected; he already knew the answer to that question without having to really think about it.

Chapter

16

ELLA SAT ON THE BENCH POSITIONED UNDERNEATH the window of Sir Almas's room and had her knees pulled up close to her chest. She drew the window curtain back and stared out at the villagers bustling up and down the streets.

Teary Isles was a strange land and the kingdom of Oak Land only seemed to add to the wonder. The people who lived there had a warm welcoming way about them, but they spoke with reserve.

She began to take notice of carriages and riders coming from other areas. She knew this by the way they dressed and customs they used.

One of the most noticeable arrivals was an entourage from another kingdom that went with a fancy carriage. The carriage stopped in the main courtyard of the city and from it emerged a nobleman and his wife. The noblemen was a tall gentlemen with dark hair and eyes, a full face and hook nose. He wore a dark blue uniform, with a pale blue sash across his chest and set on this sash was a golden dragon head. His cloak was dark blue and fringed with white rabbit fur around the collar and at his side was a golden handled sword.

He helped a gorgeous auburn-haired woman from the carriage. She wore a handsome maroon gown with a white lace bodice and cuffs. Around her delicate ivory neck was a golden chain adorned with a sapphire crystal. The woman radiated with warmth and kept a tireless smile on her face.

A wagon behind the noblemen's carriage, was filled with their personal belongings and servants that attended them. Two mounted soldiers remained at the head of the carriage carrying banners from that kingdom.

Della was able to make out the color and name on the banners. The banners were dark blue with a snarling golden dragon's head in the upper left corner and the name in bold black letters read: **'Brooklyn Falls.'**

Behind the servant's wagon stood a half dozen foot soldiers dressed in the same dark blue and grey chainmail, along with open-face helmets that had blue plumes coming from the tops. Still behind these soldiers were four mounted knights in plate mail and they carried long spears.

When the noblemen and his wife arrived the Baron of Oak Land and his family turned out to welcome them in.

Della marveled at the colorful garb of this kingdom and how friendly their ruler was. The exchange between the leaders was warm and cordial, nothing like this ever happened in her home kingdom of Millet.

How strange these people and their customs are. She observed.

Her thoughts seemed to ramble wildly throughout her mind going over the events of the past few weeks.

Why was I brought? Why is the knight being so kind to me? What does he want with me?

She was overwhelmed and uncertain of the kindness the knight and his sister showed toward her. She could not remember the last time such gentleness was shown to her.

She was scared.

What if the knight grew tired of her and sold her? Was this his intentions the entire time?

Could he really be so cruel as to be lying to her the whole time?

She had seen it all before, she would not be surprised if it were happening to her again. Since the death of her parents she had not known anyone to tell the truth or show kindness unless it was a mask to conceal their true, often sinister agendas.

Outside she gazed at a half-starved group of young children running about playing with carefree ease. Some children were rough housing each other, while others kicked a ball around and two worked at swordplay with willow sticks.

They were dirty, clothes were torn, and hung in rags from the children's bony frames. All were barefooted, marred with a number of scars and bruises, and many had their hair cropped short, both boys and girls.

Even though they were hungry and wondering where their next meal would come from, and yet they played with joyful bliss and innocence.

Why were they so happy? What was there to be joyful about when their bellies were empty? Della pondered curiously.

Watching the children made Della long to feel like they did. She wanted to know what it was like to be at peace and be as happy as the children in the street. It made her long for something she had never experienced. Her childhood was robbed from her when she was four and placed into the slave trade.

What does it mean not to live in fear? Not to be scared of everything being torn away from you in the blink of an eye.

To know what it felt like to live freely.

After the death of her parents she had grown up in a world filled with betrayals and abuse. Never had she known kindness or love. To so many people she had encountered throughout her life, they saw her only as property—lower than dirt.

All her life she had been nothing.

Tears began to well in her eyes as she thought back to weeks before when she was still a slave in the camp of the army of Millet.

Oh, how she felt so trapped at the time with no conceivable way out of that life, but death. The misery was a crushing weight that she had carried around with her for so long that she could bear it no more. Only then when she felt at the end of everything did hope to come to her.

The knight had come into her world and stopped her from taking her own life.

Someone cared about **her**.

How was that possible, how could she mean anything to him when he did not even know her? What was she to him?

Wiping the tears away, Della brushed the thought away and got up off the bench turning toward the room. It was larger than anything Della had ever seen—and she had it all to herself. The very idea was still strange to her, but she knew that she had slept there the night before.

Sometimes, she feared that it all was an elaborate wonderful dream and she would wake up at any moment to find that she was still a slave in the camp of Millet. Della had learned long ago not to take anything for granted. Whenever you started to get used to something; it was always taken away.

Sighing deeply, Della crept as soundlessly as possible across the room and peaked out of the door into the room beyond. All was silent and Amelia was nowhere to be found; presumably out running some errands.

Odd, the knight trusts me enough to leave me on my own in his house. He's not worried about me possibly running away. Della thought to herself feeling a little puzzled by the knight's actions.

Slowly, she left the security of the bedroom and made her way over to the shelf in the main room; that had trinkets lined up on it. One item stuck out to her more than all the others. It was the figurine of a woman in flowing robes, she held both hands to her face and bowed her head sobbing. She recognized the statue and recalled the legend that went along with the fashioning of it.

Teary Isles had the tale that the country got its namesake, because a mother who mourned the loss of her seven sons that ventured into the untamed land and all disappeared. Some believed that her spirit haunted the Cora Sea, between Teary Isles and Varamor. They said in the storms when the wind began to howl you could hear the wailing sobs of a woman, and they were convinced it was the sonless mother of the seven.

Della had only seen one other statue, but it was badly damaged from being taken as captured loot by the army of Millet and they only wanted to sell it, because it was made from pure silver and black steel.

The statue the knight owned was like new.

How did he get one of these? They are rumored to have only been given to the royal family members of Teary Isles. Della wondered as she reached for it. *It is so beautiful…*

With gentle hands of caution, she picked it up off its place on the shelf. She stroked the smooth shiny silver figure.

Suddenly, Della heard movement at the front door. Quickly, she set the statue back in its place on the shelf and dashed off to the safety of the knight's room. When she closed the door behind her, she left it open just a crack so she could see who came in.

Amelia came through the front door carrying an arm load of food goods and a young lad came in behind her carrying more household goods. The young boy placed the items on the table before Amelia gave him a few coins and sent him on his way.

"I'm home!" she announced taking her shawl off. "Hello?"

Della froze in place at the end of the bed; unable to move or breathe. Part of her wanted to go out and meet Amelia, but the strongest part of her that was afraid prevented her from moving a muscle. She was never sure if people were going to be kind to her or hurt her.

She feared being placed on the auction block…again.

"Hey, are you here?" Amelia asked walking hesitantly toward her brother's room.

Quickly, Della backed away from the door before she turned and ran for the bed. She flipped the covers back and jumped into the bed and pulled the protective covers over her head.

"Miss?" Amelia asked pushing the door open.

When Amelia saw that the young woman was in bed with the covers drawn up over her head, she silently backed out of the room and pulled the door shut quietly behind her.

Deep down, Della wished she weren't so fearful.

When Sir Almas came home well after dark; both Amelia and the young woman sat at the table eating supper.

Coming home was brightened with a new occupant living in their home. Sir Almas was beginning to look forward to the young woman's company—something he would have never imagined would have been possible.

He only hoped that the council would rule in his favor and allow the young woman to continue to stay with them.

Chapter

17

"How was your day?" Amelia asked passing the bowl of potatoes across to Sir Almas.

"Annoying, tiring, and I never—never want to see another fabric listing ever again." Sir Almas said shaking his head in disgust.

"There must be a lot of cataloging to do after two years." His sister remarked.

"You said it." He agreed dishing up.

"So, how was the day for the two of you?" he asked looking over at Della.

"Quite good. I went to the market and picked up enough supplies for the rest of the season." Amelia replied eagerly.

Sir Almas inadvertently tuned his sister out as he was again taken by the beauty of the young woman seated across from him.

The young woman sat in perfect silence; her back stiff as a board while she picked at her potatoes and kept her eyes down.

He knew that she was listening but figured that she was taught never to look up into the faces of other people because she had been a slave.

He studied the way her raven black hair flowed down over her shoulders and back. Her narrow chin and cheeks; her timid gentle mannerisms. She was uncommonly beautiful, even being as skinny and frightened as she was.

"Almas? Almas?!" his sister exclaimed in a tone of annoyance. "Are you even listening to me?"

"Huh? What—um, yes." Sir Almas stumbled snapping back to reality as he tore his gaze away from the young woman to look at his sister.

"Yes, yes, I am listening."

"No, you are not." Amelia stated flatly.

"I am sorry, Amelia. I drew a blank for a moment there." Sir Almas apologized.

"Right," his sister snorted with a doubtful look on her face.

"Please, Amelia, will you forgive me?" her brother asked sincerely.

"It's fine, it wasn't important anyways." She said dismissively.

"Please, tell me about your day again. I promise I will listen better this time."

"I have to go get ready; Toby will be meeting me at the market square this evening. If I don't leave soon, I'll be late." Amelia said ignoring her brother's plead as she wiped her lips on her napkin and got up from the table. "Enjoy the meal and don't worry about the cleanup, I'll do it when I get home later."

Sir Almas watched his sister as she marched off toward her bedroom in a huff. Sighing in frustrated annoyance, he threw his fork down on his plate and ran his hands over his face. His fork made a loud clank as it struck the edge of his plate making Della jump in fearful surprise. She felt petrified and awkward being in the presence of the two siblings while they were fighting with each other.

She felt like running out of the room and hiding underneath the protective blanket of the knight's bed, she wanted to disappear at that moment.

"Why do we always have to do this," the knight mumbled placing his hands palms down on the tabletop. "Every single time."

Della peaked over at the knight from the corner of her eyes. It was the first time she had ever seen him red-faced angry and deeply upset. Clenching his hands into fists, he pushed his chair back, got up and strode off in the direction of his sister's room. Della sat alone in the silent room; she could hear the voice of the knight and his sister as it carried from the bedroom in muffled rumbles.

"Why are you so upset with me?" Sir Almas demanded his voice becoming clear as Amelia opened her door.

"I'm not upset with you."

"Yes, you are."

"Look, Almas, just let it go." His sister appealed as she took a few steps into the main room.

"How can I when you won't tell me why your so upset. You know it will eat at me all night knowing I have made you unhappy." Her brother reasoned earnestly.

"No," Amelia refused through clenched teeth as she looked down.

"Amelia," Sir Almas' tone was firm.

"All right, do you really want to know why I am upset?" Amelia scoffed furiously.

"It's because of **her**!"

As she said this, she pointed over to the young woman sitting at the table. Amelia's words and actions caused Della to sink lower in her chair, until she became eye-level with the tabletop.

"What? You mean the girl?" Sir Almas gasped in surprise, looking at his sister in disbelief.

"Yes! You brought her here, to our home—into our lives without asking me first! We both live in his house, don't you remember?!" Amelia snapped looking up at Sir Almas.

"You are so obsessed with her and give her all your attention that I might as well not exist!"

"That is not true."

"Isn't it? How about tonight?" Amelia ranted. "During supper you couldn't take your eyes off of her."

Sir Almas remained silent.

"What is so important about her and why do you feel that you have to be responsible for her?" his sister demanded.

"Because, she has no one else." He replied in a low tone.

"So do the other girls the army brought back here, how is she any different?"

Again, Sir Almas did not answer her.

"You don't even know why, do you?" Amelia huffed rolling her eyes. "I have to go. We will finish this discussion later."

As Della sat at the table and heard the arguing ensue, after the two of them disappeared into Amelia's room. The last thing she wanted was to be the cause of the family fighting or possible division.

Right now, all she wanted to do was to vanish away.

I should have never come with him. Della thought mournfully.

"Why do you always run away when we are having a serious discussion?" Sir Almas demanded in annoyance.

They reemerged from the room minutes later, Amelia stomped haughtily away from her brother and the knight pursued her, his expression drawn.

"I am not running away." Amelia defended as she grabbed her shawl off the hook by the door.

"Yes, you are." Almas's words punctuated the air.

Amelia turned to her brother and she opened her mouth to respond, but closed it again when she looked past him to Della.

"Look, I have to go." she muttered opening the door and slipped out, leaving her brother standing there.

Sir Almas groaned aloud with frustration and rubbed his hand over his face.

"Why? Why now?" he muttered under his breath.

He abruptly turned around, the anger was still evident on his face, until his eyes locked on the young woman. The angry look on his face disappeared and was replaced by a soft embarrassed look.

"I-ah…" he trailed off at a loss for words.

Before he had a chance to say anything more, the young woman slipped out of her chair and rushed to his room in fear and closed the door behind her.

She jumped onto the bed and crawled under the safety and security of the bear skin blanket.

Chapter

18

THE TENSE MOOD AROUND THE HOUSE CARRIED ON FOR the next few days. Neither Sir Almas or Amelia spoke to each other, they passed through the house in silence, and they ate their meals alone.

Della would hide in the bedroom until they both left the house. She felt so out of place and ashamed about being there, knowing that she was the cause of the division between them. She had conformation in her assumption that both brother and sister did not want her around, because Sir Almas had not uttered a single word to her since the night he and his sister fought.

During the day hours, Della would sit at the window bench of the knight's room and watch the world going on outside. She was fond of how happy and free the children were; never in all her life had she seen such happy children and the villagers went about their business with a similar ease. Oak Land seemed like a constant peaceful place, where most everyone went on about their daily lives without seeming to worry.

She wished she could be a part of that world.

Deep down, though, she knew she could never really be a part of this land. It was not so much the fact that these people weren't hers or that this land was strange, but it was because she was different. She had been a prisoner of another life; beaten, hated, and viciously abused. Everything was different now; she was free. But she did not know what to do with freedom…she did not know what it really was. She had been a slave for so long that it was difficult for her to believe that she was free and being cared for.

When this possibility rose, Della was brought back to the conflict that was going on in the Martin home. Brother and sister were at odds with each other—and she was to blame.

Maybe it will be for the better if I leave. Della pondered seriously. *I am unhappy and I have caused so much strife all ready. If I stay it will only get worse.*

It was late in the afternoon and she knew that the knight would be coming home soon because it was the time of the fall festival in Oak Land. Sir Almas was helping with the setup and organization of the events, which made it so that he would come home earlier than usual. Amelia wouldn't be back until later that night, she spent much of her time seeing the sights of the festival and helping the Priest sell baked goods to raise coin for the shelter for orphans and refugees.

If Della was going to have the best time to run away, it was now. If she was gone Sir Almas and Amelia could go back to getting along and being a family again. Their lives would not be upset or inconvenienced by her presence anymore.

They would be better off without her.

Making her mind up; Della got up off the bench and started for the door of the room. With slow hesitant steps she made her way to the front door and opened it. She paused at the threshold before she stepped out into the world and let the door close behind her with a soft thud.

The sun was shining warmly on her face and shoulders. The air was filled with smells of smoke from roasting meat, dirt, and other fall aromas. The children that played in the street, stared at her with mouths agape and eyes of wonder as she stumbled past them.

She was different and even though she was dressed similarly to them, they knew she was not native to their kingdom. The villagers gave her strange looks, while others frown at her in disapproval. Some of the street children were overcome with curiosity and began to follow the young woman as she made her way through the streets and alleys. They spoke to each other in hushed whispers, while others laughed and danced around her.

At first, she did not pay them mind, but gradually the group began to grow and fill with older children and they closed in around her. She was beginning to feel overwhelmed and uneasy about the nearness of so many strangers.

"She's one of those foreigners," a boy announced.

"You mean one of those the army brought back with them?" a little girl asked.

"Yeah!" another boy eagerly filled in. "A slave!"

"She's one of the invaders!" a cruel girl sneered.

"Invader! Invader!" they began to chant. "Go away! You're not wanted, invader!"

Della began to get an inkling of fear deep down as they continued to chant with sinister looks on their faces and danced closer around her.

Suddenly, a clump of mud came flying out of the crowd of children and struck Della in the shoulder. Taking this as their cue, the other children began their attack, using mud, and stones on Della. Yelling angry insults at her, they threw their projectiles.

"Invader! Invader!"

"Go away!"

Stones and mud painfully struck her, arms, legs, and back. Della held her arms over her head and face to block out as much of the objects as she could. She broke into a stumbling run running for a shadowy empty looking alley. The children kept pursuing her and the crowd only seemed to grow in size.

Tears of pain and fear ran down Della's face as she ran along trying to get away from her vicious attackers. She weaved through the alleys, side streets, and around many buildings; no matter what she did she could seem to escape the mob.

Della emerged onto the open market area. Market goers and booth owners stopped what they were doing and stared at the scene that was taking place. She became cornered when she was faced with a well on one side and a booth selling vegetables on the other.

"Get her!" a vicious boy encouraged.

The ever-growing crowd of children surrounded her and threw their dangerous projectiles at her. Feeling the impact of the objects hitting her, she was brought to her knees. At strong defiant feeling of anger welled in her; such an anger that she hadn't felt since the day she was in the camp of the Millet army when Oak Land's soldiers came to rescue them.

She would be silent no longer.

"Leave me alone!" she screamed.

Her strongly accented voice rang throughout the marketplace. The sudden outburst from Della made the attacking children stop short and drop the rest of their weapons, staring at her in startled shock.

They did not expect her to fight back.

"Leave me alone!" she screamed again as she rose to her feet, fists clenched at her sides and glared at everyone around her.

Glancing at the older people the children turned and split in all direction for dread of getting in trouble. Della stood alone among the strangers and they stared at her with their critical judgmental eyes. Some turned to each other and whispered as they pointed toward Della.

"She's a foreigner." a woman hissed.

"From the Forbidden Lands—she doesn't belong here." a man said frowning.

"Look at the brand on the side of her head. She's a slave!" a plump woman called out in horror.

"Where did she come from?"

"How did she get here?"

"I wonder who she belongs to?"

All these questions bubbled through the gawking crowd as they looked upon Della. Feeling terribly out of place she moved in the direction of the main street, but stopped because there was a wall of people in front of her. She tried to rush away from the group of people, but they were in every direction she turned.

She felt like a wild animal caught in a trap.

Forcing her way through a small line of people, Della was clear of the market crowd and she broke into a run again.

She dodged around villagers, carts, horses, and soldiers. It seemed that everyone she passed would only stare at her, knowing that she was a stranger in their land.

She did not belong—she never would.

Della felt like the walls of the city were closing in on her, the air felt suffocating, and she was filled with the desperate feeling of needing to escape.

I have to get out of here! I don't belong! Della screamed inwardly, overcome with panic.

She kept looking about in petrified fear; half expecting the mob of children to turn up again and attack her. Della was lost and had no idea where the knight's house was; she could not go back and hide under the safe covers of the bed, even if she wanted to.

She had made her choice—there was no going back now.

Coming around a sharp bend in the alley she was running down, she saw that the main gate of the city stood five hundred feet away. It was drawn open as the people move into and out of it on their daily business.

Feeling a small twinge of relief; Della saw her chance.

Freedom.

She dashed for it, ignoring everyone and anything around her. She had no plan for when she got on the other side of the gate, all she knew was that she wanted to get away from all these cruel people.

When she was several yards from the open world, a voice suddenly rang out.

"Wait—stop!"

She instantly froze in place, recognizing the tone of that voice. It was Sir Almas.

A trial period?" the knight question with a tone of annoyance.

"Yes," Priest Lumis said patiently.

He walked beside the knight as they made their way down the street nearing the poorer district where the knight lived. Sir Almas had invited the Priest over for supper that evening so he could meet with the young woman for the second time and he could get the older man's opinion on her. The visit would also serve the purpose of bringing information back to the council regarding the young woman living under the knight's care.

"They are not against you taking her on as your ward, but they want to be sure the arrangement will work out and that the young woman is settling in." the Priest explained.

"You mean they want to make sure the girl isn't causing any inconvenience for their precious people and city." the knight muttered in a bitter tone. "Or to be certain that we aren't doing—"

"Almas, please!" Priest Lumis cried his eyes widening at the direction the conversation was taking.

"Pardon me," Sir Almas apologized lowering his head, ashamed. "I don't mean to offend you, but I know how most of the council members think. They believe that everyone else lives as loosely as they do."

"As do I, but that doesn't mean you have to paint me a picture." the Priest muttered shuttering.

"I know how offended and upset you are by the actions of the council, but you must learn to be patient. I am certain it will all work out for the best."

"Even if it means letting them possibly decide to have her sent away?"

"Yes, even that." the Priest spoke in a wise tone.

Sir Almas looked off into the distance down the street. He did not want to even think of the possibility that the council could order the young woman to be sent away to the refugee home.

"Almas," the Priest spoke to him in the way that he did when the knight was a small boy.

The knight looked down at the ground, but didn't say a word.

"You can't let her go, can you?"

"No...I don't suppose I can." Sir Almas admitted letting out a heaving sigh. "The girl is no longer just someone to help. She's become much more than that."

"Oh? In what way?" Priest Lumis probed expectantly.

"She's family, Lumis." Sir Almas said looking at the Priest with earnest eyes. "Amelia and I have grown used to having her around the house. She's like having a little sister."

"So, her leaving would not only be difficult for you to take, but it would be hard on Amelia as well?" Priest Lumis asked with a look of surprise.

"Yes," Sir Almas replied with a tone of hesitancy.

"But more for you, I suspect." The Priest said with a knowing look.

"Excuse me?"

"Come now, Almas." Priest Lumis said stopping and faced the knight.

"Since the day I came to visit after you got home, I saw how you were around the young woman. Just admit it, Almas, you are taken with the girl."

"What are you implying?" the knight took offense.

"I imply nothing, only stating what I have come to observe," the Priest replied coolly before he went on.

"Fret not. I will tell no other. Besides, I feel it is good to see you have someone to care for. Especially with your sister soon to be wed and leaving the house..."

The Priest's attention was roused when he noticed that the knight wasn't listening to him anymore, but looking down the street with a startled expression on his face.

"What is it?" Priest Lumis asked looking down the street.

When he looked toward the main thoroughfare of the castle where the gate was, he saw a woman running down the lane. He was perplexed by the look of alarmed surprise on the knight's face.

"Almas? Almas, do you know who that is?" the Priest asked the distracted man.

Without answering, the knight started at a jog down the street toward the running woman; the genuine concern was evident in his mannerisms.

"Wait—stop!" he shouted.

Chapter

19

"PLEASE, WAIT!" THE KNIGHT PLEADED.

Stopping short, Della slowly turned around and faced the knight. Sir Almas stood several feet away and he was breathing hard from the effort of running. Behind him Priest Lumis came hurrying toward them, as always, he had a kind warm expression on his face.

She saw in the knight's eyes something she never thought she ever would.

It was fear.

"Please, don't leave," he said gently. "I know your scared and upset. I...I am sorry that Amelia and I have been fighting. I want you to know that it's not in any way your fault..."

When Della stood before him, she did not feel like running away—she felt safe knowing the knight was there. The knight grimaced when he looked her up and down and saw how dirty, bruised, and cut up she was.

"I am sorry. I wish you did not have to be put through all of that," the knight apologized, looking ashamed.

"You are not seriously hurt, are you?"

When he asked this, he took a step toward her.

"N—not badly." the young woman replied.

The knight stopped short and stared at her in stunned silence. It was the first time the young woman had willingly answered him, and it hadn't been a threat either. For Della, she felt there was no point to holding her silence, the knight was being kind to her despite everything she had been putting him through.

"Were you running away?" Sir Almas asked puzzled.

"Yes," Della gave a nod.

"Why?" he sounded hurt.

"You and your sister were fighting," Della reasoned looking down at her feet. "Amelia is upset with you because of me…I am dividing your family."

"That is not true," he told her shaking his head. "Amelia and I have many disagreements, this last one is no different. She has never liked it when I am away on missions for the kingdom, we quibble almost every time I return home."

Della looked up at him with a look of unconvinced puzzlement.

"He is telling you the truth," Priest Lumis assured her with a solemn nod.

Della frowned thoughtfully as her gaze drifted back over to the knight.

"There are times when we won't speak to each other for weeks." the knight added.

"You are not the problem—and you never will be."

"Amelia is mad at you because of me." Della said at almost a whisper.

"Amelia is only jealous," the knight sharply countered. "She's truly a wonderfully sweet woman, but at times she thinks the world revolves around her. She considers you as competition for my affection."

"That is why I cannot stay," Della replied looking down shamefully. "I am making her unhappy."

"But I don't want you to go." the knight spoke up. "Doesn't what I want matter?"

Della looked up at him in surprised.

"I—I don't want you to go, because…I really care about you."

"Please, just give staying with us a chance," Sir Almas begged earnestly. "Amelia won't be living at the cottage for very long. Soon she and Toby will be wed, and she will move out. Don't you see? You won't have to worry about upsetting her."

Della seriously pondered his offer, part of her wanted to leave; for his sake and to make it so that there would be peace between him and his sister once more. Without her around, she knew that Amelia would be happy and in turn so would the knight.

Yet, at the same time, she knew that she didn't know anything about the country of Teary Isles and if she tried to go off on her own, either she would end up in deep trouble or wouldn't last long.

Staying in the Martin's household was her best possibility… for now.

"I…I will stay." she said slowly.

"Very well," Sir Almas replied sounding relieved. "Come with me, I'll take you home."

Home.

It was such a strange word for a place that she hardly new. But, there was something comforting in the words and the tone of his voice. Hesitantly, the knight opened his hand and offered it out for her to take.

With uncertain slow steps, Della walked toward the knight and slipped her trembling hand into his. His grip was soft and gentle, he did not fully close his hand around hers so she could pull away anytime she wanted to. He didn't pull her along either, but stood where he was and waited for her to walk beside him willingly.

After all he had been put through by her and everything she had done to make things difficult for him, he remained kind and forgiving.

All I have been is ungrateful and difficult to be around. Della pondered feeling guilty.

How can he choose to be continuously kind and patient with me, when I have only repaid him with bitter cruelty?

Della stood there; her gaze locked on his kind smiling face. She pondered what she could offer to the knight in return for his generosity and kindness. Then the thought occurred to her; ever since he had encountered her in the camp of Millet, all he ever asked of her was to know her name.

What purpose was it serving to keep it a secret?

"Della…" she whispered softly.

"Excuse me?" Sir Almas asked giving her his full attention.

"M—my name," she said dropping her eyes to the ground.

"My name is Della Metsula."

Sir Almas' mouth dropped open; he could hardly believe what he had just heard. A wide smile spread across his face and he felt like leaping and shouting for joy. Looking over his shoulder he saw that the Priest was smiling heartily, understanding how much knowing the young woman's name meant to the knight.

A look of fascinated wonder spread over his face as he gazed back onto the woman.

"Della Metsula," he uttered slowly. "What a beautiful name."

Della blushed at his compliment, but tried to mask it by putting a hand to her cheek and turned her face away.

"Now, I finally have something to call you," he announced with pride. "Such a delightful name."

"Don't you think so, Priest Lumis?"

"Aye, I do." Priest Lumis agreed with a nod of approval. "I believe Della means, *angelic* and Metsula is *strong* in the language of Varamor."

Della nodded in response.

"My, my," Sir Almas gasped overtaken by amazement. "Angelically Strong."

Della's cheeks went uncontrollably flush at the knight's praise.

"Almas, I think you are embarrassing her." Priest Lumis said taking notice of Della's flush cheeks.

"Pardon me, Della." he apologized. "I didn't mean to make you feel uncomfortable."

"Perhaps, we should be heading to your place before the night sets in," the Priest suggested as he glanced around.

"Night festivities will begin soon, and things can get pretty wild out here."

"Um…of course." the knight stumbled as he blinked a few times and pulled his eyes away from the young woman.

Together the three of them started out on their way again, beginning a new chapter in their relationship.

Chapter
20

Once they got back to the knight's home, Priest Lumis set to work preparing the evening meal while the knight helped the young woman get cleaned up and treated her injuries.

"Will you stay for the night or are you going to the festival?" Della whispered timidly.

She watched the knight as he brought her the second dress that Amelia had given to her. Della looked at the faded blue long sleeved dress and could not help frowning with distaste at the fashion.

"I know you're not used to wearing clothes like this, but until we can get to market and pick up some new ones, these will have to do." the knight reasoned seeing her reaction to the dress.

Della nodded somberly as she took the dress from the knight.

The dress had a clasp together front bodice, with white lace around the bottom of the sleeves, and neckline. Immediately, Della knew she hated the length of the dress, it would have the same problem for her as the last one, she kept tripping on the skirt and didn't like to have to lift it to keep it out of the dust.

"Let me know when you are dressed." the knight said before he backed out of the bedroom and gently closed the door behind him.

He did not answer my question.

Draping the dress over the bed, she looked at it thoughtfully, before an idea struck her.

Sir Almas had been pacing back in forth in front of the door, mulling over how he was going to answer the young woman's inquiry. He had a feeling that she would not like it that he was going to have to head back out again that evening. He had to replace Captain Toby on duty to make sure that the festival goers celebrating did not get out of hand.

Imagine me worrying about how I am going to explain myself? It was never like this with Amelia. the knight reflected. *But then again, Amelia was my sister, Della on the other hand is different…special.*

He heard the door latch click and the door was slowly drawn open. Turning toward the room, all he could do was stand there and stare in awe.

Della stood at the threshold of the room, looking timid and uncertain. The knight found that he could not help smiling with amusement at what she had done to the dress.

The young woman had cut the dress off at the knees and was barefooted underneath. Also, she had torn the sleeves off just above the elbows.

"I see you made some changes." he remarked stifling a chuckle.

"It was too long." she replied simply.

"I like it." He approved. "Suits you better."

It more than just suited her better, she was stunning. Sir Almas enjoyed it when she did things such as this, he knew in a way it was helping her get her independence back. Inside he was smiling like a fool, but he kept his facial expressions to a minimum knowing how easily the young woman became embarrassed.

The young woman bowed her head slightly in acknowledgement.

"Shall we go see if Priest Lumis needs any help with the meal?" the knight asked motioning toward the kitchen area.

When they got over to the cooking area, Priest Lumis had the table all set and was frying the fish that they brought home from the market with them.

"Do you need a hand?" Sir Almas inquired.

"No, but I thank you for the offer," the Priest said kindly as he turned and smiled at them.

When he saw what Della was wearing, he raised a brow, but did not utter a word.

"When do you have to head out again?" the Priest asked wiping his fingers on his apron.

"Pretty soon." the knight said with a sigh.

He wished more than anything now that he could stay here with the Priest and Della for the night. Finding out the young woman's name set him in such a high mood that he wanted to see if he could speak further to her.

But alas, duty called!

"Do you have time to sit and eat?"

"I'm afraid not," Sir Almas replied frowning. "Toby will probably be wondering where I have gotten off to."

"Hmm, I suppose he and your sister will be going out to enjoy the festivities tonight?" Priest Lumis asked with interest.

"Yes," the knight nodded

"Well, don't worry," the Priest assured him. "I can stay here with the young woman, until you or your sister returns…if you wish."

"Would you?" Sir Almas asked earnestly. "I mean, if you wouldn't mind."

"I would be delighted to. It would give me a chance to get to know her a little better. This way she won't have to be alone."

"That would be just perfect," the knight said relieved. "Thank you, Priest Lumis."

"Um…" the knight looked to the young woman and paused, feeling a little awkward.

"Would that be all right with you, Della?"

Both men expectantly turned their attention toward the young woman. She froze in place; she had never been given the choice of deciding what she wanted.

She did not know what to do or how to respond.

"What would you like?" Priest Lumis asked softly.

Della nervously nibbled on her bottom lip, trying to think through the fog that enveloped her mind at that very moment. She looked at the Priest; she did not get a feeling of fear being around the elderly man. She felt that if the knight trusted the man, then she might also be able to do the same.

"It's all right, Della." Sir Almas reassured her. "Priest Lumis is a good kind man and he will take diligent care of you until I get back. He helped take care of Amelia and I after our parents died during the Keltar Nor Wars.

You can trust him; he will not harm you."

Taking a deep breath, Della nodded her head in consent.

"I am safe now," she replied looking back into the comforting face of the knight. "I will stay here with the Priest."

"Good, good." Sir Almas said smiling.

"Don't worry, I should be back some time after midnight." he said as he buckled his sword back around his waist.

"I think you and Priest Lumis shall have a good time together. Perhaps, you can spend it getting to know one another."

Della and the Priest both nodded in unison.

"Okay, I'll be off." the knight said in a hurried tone as he headed for the door.

"Just one more thing," he noted stopping to face them, worry etched in his eyes. "Please, try not to wander off like that ever again...okay?"

"I won't." Della replied, truly meaning it.

"Good," Sir Almas said. "See you later. Thanks again, Priest Lumis."

Della slightly raised a hand and waved her fingers to the knight.

Seeing this gesture from the young woman, only made the knight smile wider as he backed his way toward the door. He grinned like an excited young boy as he stumbled over his own feet while walking backward.

Della laughed inwardly at the knight's antics as the man fumbled his way out the door, she could hardly believe that the knight could make her feel the way she did right then. She actually felt happy and relaxed, a feeling she thought she had lost.

"Well, shall we get started?" Priest Lumis asked once the knight was gone.

Della turned back to the Priest as he began to flip the fish to brown on the other side, and he offered her a plate to hold for him to dish the fish out onto once they were finished cooking.

Chapter

21

A FEW DAYS LATER AND THE FALL FESTIVAL WAS IN full swing. Representatives from nearly every kingdom in Teary Isles were in attendance. These kingdoms brought some of their best champions to take part in the games.

The champions were going to be competing for a wreath crown made from silver and the title of festival champion. The winner would be hailed throughout Teary Isles and go on a tour through each kingdom bearing the title of greatest knight in all the land for a whole year.

There was also a sizable purse for the winner of the festival games, and small winnings for those who won their specialty division. Sir Almas was eager to take part in the games because of the purse money that he knew could set them up for a year and he would have enough left over to give Amelia a sizeable dowry.

Amelia was not keen on the whole idea.

"Almas, I wish you would quit attending these games." she complained fretfully.

"I'll be fine, sister." the knight assured her as he dressed in his ceremonial armor.

"Oh, really?" Amelia challenged crossing her arms.

"Do you remember what happen at the last festival games? You broke your wrist during jousting, and it has never been right since."

"It was that one time, Amelia." Sir Almas reasoned rolling his eyes. "Besides, it hasn't bothered me for months."

"Almas, as your sister, I am begging you not to partake in the games." Amelia pleaded close to tears.

"Amelia, I want to do this more than anything right now," Sir Almas insisted earnestly as he looked at her. "I have been away from home for so long and missed so much. The games are my favorite part of the festival. Aside from that the purse money is good."

Amelia gave him a look of annoyed frustration, tapping her toe on the floor.

"It's ten pieces of silver for the winner of each match and if I can win the title it would mean a silver crown and a hundred pieces of gold. Do you know how far that much coinage could take us?" he said willingly.

"We don't need the money," Amelia argued. "You make plenty enough from your commission as a knight."

"Very well, I will do it out of pure enjoyment." he said pulling his dark green tunic over his head.

"Please, just let me have this one enjoyment, please Amelia."

"All right, fine!" Amelia said in exasperation throwing her hands in the air.

"But don't expect me to support you—or watch any of your matches."

"Don't worry." Sir Almas muttered not hiding his sarcasm as he buckled his sword on. "I never do."

Amelia scowled at her brother before turning on her heels and strode into her room flinging herself down on the bed in anger.

Sir Almas ignored his sister's behavior as he went into his room before emerging moments later carrying his good cloak. Della sat on the floor of the main room near the fireplace hemming up the dress she cut short.

"Della?" Sir Almas asked stopping near the young woman.

She looked up at the knight with innocent fawn eyes.

"Would you like to accompany me to the opening ceremony of the festival games?"

Della sat thoughtful for a moment and decided that it would be better than sitting around the house sewing or having to be around the knight's grumpy sister.

"Okay," she said with a nod.

"Good," Sir Almas said smiling, "Can you help me carry a few things?"

Once again, Della nodded readily.

"Could you go and get my pack over by the table?" he asked kindly. "It has the rest of the gear I will need for the games later today."

Della set her sewing aside, got up from the floor and headed across the room to the table. She picked the heavy pack up off the floor and slung it over her shoulder and grabbed the knight's helmet up off the table before heading back over to him.

"Thank you," he said gratefully. "I nearly forgot about my helmet."

When she got up beside the knight, he took his helmet from her and tucked it underneath his arm.

"We will see you tonight, Amelia." He informed his sister opening the front door.

Sir Almas lingered at the door, but his sister never uttered a sound. He was visibly upset, clenching his jaw, he groaned and shook his head in disgust.

"Let's be off." He told Della as he held the door open for her.

Della stepped out the door ahead of him and waited for him to close the door behind them. Once that was done, he began leading the way down the street and she fell into step close at his side.

After the opening ceremonies of the games, Sir Almas entered the tent that belonged to the champions competing for the title. He found an open square where a chair, cot, stand for a suit of armor and table were.

"You can just set the pack on the cot." He told Della as he laid his shield against a support pole of the tent.

The other competitors stood around gawking at Sir Almas and the young woman in wonder and amazement. Sir Almas knew that having the young woman was drawing attention because it was not usual to have the company of a woman in the tent of the competitors. What added to this was the fact that Della was not a native of Teary Isles.

Sir Almas ignored their gazes of curiosity as he came over to the cot and knelt beside it. Opening the pack, he pulled his bracers, gloves, and bandage wraps out.

"Can you help me?" he asked holding the two bandage rolls up along with his gloves.

Nodding, Della sat down on the cot near the knight and took the wraps from him.

"I use these to protect my hands from getting chaffed and blistered during the combat matches." he explained.

Being able to help Sir Almas made Della feel good, she felt that she was able to help pay back the kindness the knight had shown her. Kneeling down in front of her, Sir Almas held one hand up for her to get started on.

Just as he opened his mouth to start explaining to her on how to wrap his hands; she began to quickly and expertly wrap them. Clapping his mouth shut, he grinned at her, marveling at how she knew so much.

"You can bind them snuggly, but not too tight." he advised. "I'll let you know if it is too tight."

"I know," she replied nodding in acknowledgement. "I have done this before."

"Of course, you have, pardon my ignorance." the knight apologized feeling embarrassed by his words.

"It's no trouble," she assured him shaking her head.

She had done tasks like this many times as a slave for the soldiers of the army of Millet and she had plenty of practice.

By the time Della had the knight's second hand wrapped and was starting on helping him slip his gloves on; a young knight came wandering closer to them.

"Hello, Malcom." Sir Almas muttered glancing up at the young man.

Della pulled his first glove on and pulled the other on, forcing herself to focus on the knight and trying to ignore how close the stranger was to her.

"A new squire? I didn't think you were the type to grab a girl." the man sneered looking the young woman over with greedy eyes.

"She's not a squire." Sir Almas muttered in an unfriendly tone. "She's a guest in my house."

"And you're making her work?"

"No, I just asked her for a little assistance. She is welcome at any time to refuse if she so chooses." the knight replied standing up.

"She's a delicious looking little thing, isn't she?" Malcom remarked taking a step forward as he reached out to stroke her hair.

"Don't!" Sir Almas warned sharply.

Snapping into action; he held his arm out in front of Della to block the other man's hand and prevent her from being touched.

"Defensive?" Malcom scoffed.

"She doesn't like to be touched." Sir Almas explained.

"Well, then, she's no fun. A spoiled thing." the knight grumbled frowning with displeasure.

"You treat her too well."

Malcom took another step toward the young woman, his hand still outstretched toward her.

"Malcom!" Sir Almas growled. "Stop!"

"Oh, come now. Let me just touch her hair." the man appealed. "It looks so smooth and...soft."

"Keep your hands away from her." the knight warned putting himself between the other man and Della.

By this time, the other men in the tent were attracted to all the commotion and began to gather around. They chuckled in amusement and egged Malcom on in his pursuit of trying to touch the young woman's hair.

"Malcom, if you don't stop now, I will be forced to hurt you!" Sir Almas threatened.

The young knight stopped short and stared at the other knight in uncertainty. Sir Almas gave him a hard-unflinching glare, fists clenched at his sides ready to snap into action.

Malcom exhaled slowly and backed away from the two of them.

"She ain't worth it." he grumbled with dissatisfaction as he turned away.

"Almas," another voice from among the other's suddenly spoke up.

The knight's head shot up and his posture stiffened at the sound of the man's voice.

"Brutus Missiani." Sir Almas addressed frowning warily.

Pushing his way through the gathering crowd was a short stocky built knight wearing richly colored clothes. His complexion was pasty white, his long brown hair was neatly comb to one side, and his beard trimmed short.

"Well, you're a sight for sore eyes." the knight declared smiling sinisterly.

"I haven't seen you at the games in a while."

"That's because I have been otherwise occupied with business of the kingdom." Sir Almas replied through grit teeth.

"Ah, I can see that." Sir Missiani remarked looking past Sir Almas to the young woman seated on the cot.

"You brought someone back with you from the campaign trail?"

"Yes," Sir Almas answered nodding slowly.

"Right, right." Sir Missiani muttered rubbing his chin thoughtfully.

"Do you recall that debt of coin you owe me?"

Sir Almas froze at mention of this, his face went white as a sheet.

"It appears that you have something that catches my fancy and that I can take as payment instead of coinage." Sir Missiani said looking at Della with greedy pleasure.

Chapter

22

"How dare you propose such a horrid thing!" Sir Almas snapped in anger.

"I have proposed nothing," Sir Missiani said easily. "I was merely making a suggestion."

"I will have the coin I owe you by the end of the month." Sir Almas informed him.

"Tell you what," Sir Missiani began with a devious look in his eyes.

"Even though you have been late by almost two years in paying your debt. I have seriously considered another way you can repay me, without added interest."

"How about this; if you win your division of sword combat, then all your debts will be forgiven, but if you should lose, you must pay me immediately—plus interest."

"You know that if I should lose, I don't have that kind of coin to pay you." Sir Almas argued.

"I know, but that is where the second part of the deal comes in." Sir Missiani countered smoothly. "Should you lose your division, instead of paying me coin you can give the girl to me instead. After all she is your servant girl…"

Sir Almas grunted loudly, the furious anger he had been holding back all came to the surface and without giving any warning he punched Sir Missiani square in the face. The other man cried out in painful surprise as he stumbled back a few feet holding a hand to his face.

"You know nothing!" Sir Almas shouted in anger.

"She is not my slave! She is a free woman, belonging to no one! What you speak is forbidden by the law of this land!"

"You!" Sir Missiani hissed holding a hand to his bloody nose.

"You will pay for this! I want my coin by the end of the festival, or I will have you thrown in prison and all your possessions confiscated!"

"You will have your precious coin and I will never have anything to do with you again!" Sir Almas shot back enraged.

"Same goes for anyone else who thinks this woman is an object to be owned or traded. I will have nothing to do with you and you best stay clear of us, understood!"

The others who had gathered around, were no longer jeering, or laughing, but had genuine looks of fear and shock on their faces. They nodded somberly and muttered under their breaths as they slowly moved away from the three.

"Curse you! Curse you, that filthy wench and your family!" Sir Missiani spat accusingly as he backed away from them.

Della was now standing behind Sir Almas, cowering in fear and too shocked by what had just transpired to speak. The knight turned around to Della with an apologetic look on his face.

"I am sorry you had to be put through that," he said offering a sincere apology.

"I can assure you that not all people are like this. Sir Missiani and I used to be good friends, but my folly was in borrowing coin from him. Doing that drove a wedge between us and ruined our friendship."

Della gave him an understanding somber nod.

"Are you okay?" he asked with deep concern. "Do you wish to return home?"

Della stood silent with a pondering expression on her face. Patiently the knight awaited her answer.

"No, I want to stay." She replied steadily.

A reassured look came over the knight's face and he allowed himself to smile slightly.

"Good, shall we finish?" he inquired nodding to the chainmail laid out on the cot.

"Of course," Della replied willingly as she approached the knight.

Quickly, and with a little struggling Della was able to help Sir Almas slip into his chainmail and put his tunic on over the chainmail. On the center of the tunic was the family crest; and image of a big horned ram fighting its way through a thicket of bloody thorns.

Della gazed at the crest in curious wonder.

"It represents the meaning of our name," he explained to her noticing her line of sight. "Martin, in the ancient Delmariean tongue means "Strong Charger" or "Unstoppable Force". Thus, my family chose the image you see before you."

"Hum, I see." Della noted nodding slowly.

"Perfect," he announced taking a breath. "I believe I am ready."

"What event are you in?" Della asked quietly.

"Ground combat, with the sword." Sir Almas said in an anxious tone.

"When do you start?" she asked.

"Soon," he responded as he picked his helmet up off the cot. "I must go and announce my entry now."

Della followed Sir Almas as he left the tent and approached the registration table near the wooden walled fight ring where combatants were already going at it. Two men dressed in robes of lavish material and design were seated behind the table. With each entry the skinner of the two would question the participant and the second man would act as scribe taking down the information given.

Already, the list on the table before the men was half full of names or marks of the knights entered in competitions.

"Name, kingdom, position, and which events you wish to compete in." the first man droned on with little interest.

"I am Sir Almas Martin, a knight of the kingdom of Oak Land. I wish to partake in the events of Jousting and Ground Combat." The knight reported standing at attention.

"Very well, sign your name." the second man acknowledged lazily.

Sir Almas stepped up to the table as the scribe turned the parchment scroll around for him and handed him the quill for Sir Almas to sign his name.

"Good luck and enjoy your games." The scribe said motioning Sir Almas on.

"Thank you." Sir Almas said with a respectful bow of his head.

"Now, we are ready." He whispered to Della as he took a deep breath.

Together, Sir Almas took Della over to the combat ring and stood in the group with the other knights preparing to compete.

The combat arena was an octagon shaped area, with high solid grey wood walls and the ground was layered a foot thick with coarse sand. Flanking the arena directly across from the entrance gate were several flag poles and attached to these poles were banners from each house.

All the banners were colorful; one was a combination of red and orange, with another was purple and red, and yet another was gold and black. Standing on a platform adjacent of the banners was the arena herald that announced each match and victor.

Around the rest of the arena was an upraised narrow board in which spectators stood on so they could look over the sides of the arena into the ring and cheer on their favorite combatant.

Della found that she did not much care for the ground combat games, especially when she saw how vicious they were to one another. After a short break at the noon hour, the second set of combatants were up, including Sir Almas.

"Priest Lumis, what a surprise to see you here." Sir Almas remarked walking up to the older man who stood near the entrance of the ring.

"Well, I ought to be," the Priest reasoned, looking down at Della he gave her a warm smile.

"I am the only one with extensive knowledge in healing practices and have the abilities to deal with any injuries—for man or beast."

"Right, how could I forget." Sir Almas gave a light chuckle. "How have you like the games so far?"

"How do you think?" the Priest challenged raising a brow. "You know I have never liked the idea of grown men going around trying to maul each other to death over coinage and personal glory."

"Oh, Priest Lumis," Sir Almas remarked shaking his head. "You are missing the fun in all of it. The challenge of seeing which man is the better skilled."

"I don't care what you want to call it," Priest Lumis grumbled. "When you boil it all down, it's about beating your opponent senseless and getting praise from those who enjoy acts of violence."

"Nice to know what you think of my pursuits." Sir Almas mumbled frowning with disappointment.

"Now, Almas," Priest Lumis appealed to him. "You have known for a great many years that I have never approved of these games, but I do understand the need for them. Men like you need to work out your frustrations and to have a little fun, these games are just a way of doing that.

You don't have to listen to the disapproving ramblings of an old man."

"I listen, Tal, because I care about what you think." Sir Almas noted giving a weak smile.

"Right, and that's why you still compete, despite my feelings about the games?" the Priest said pointedly, but a smile played at the edges of his mouth.

"Yep, but its more than that." the knight replied with a shrug.

"I compete because I love it."

Priest Lumis nodded solemnly in agreement and understanding.

"I see, you're up next." the Priest noted looking at the listing board.

"That I am." the knight confirmed with a nod of his head.

"I am wondering if you wouldn't mind doing a small favor for me?"

"Anything," the Priest replied.

"Could you watch over Della for me while I compete?" Sir Almas asked nodding to the young woman standing quietly beside him.

"You've had a little trouble bringing her along, haven't you?" Priest Lumis guessed.

"Yes, but they were the usual troublemakers." Sir Almas assured him pursing his lips.

"Sir Brutus Missiani, I suppose."

"Him...among others."

"Don't worry, the young lady can stay with me," Priest Lumis reassured him. "Fret not, I will not allow anything to happen to her."

"Good, thank you, Priest Lumis," the knight said gratefully. "I owe you."

"You owe me nothing," Priest Lumis told him firmly shaking his head.

"I am delighted to have the company. Right, Miss Della?"

The Priest looked at her and warmly smiled, looking shyly up at the old man, Della gave a small smile of agreement.

"Very well, I better get to the gate, they'll be starting soon." Sir Almas said slipping his helmet on.

"See you in a little while."

"Best of luck—and God be with you my lad." the Priest wished wistfully.

"Thanks." the knight nodded to the Priest and smiling proudly at the young woman, taking in her beauty before he turned and went on his way.

For some strange reason, Della found that she was feeling incredibly nervous and worried about the knight going into the ring to compete. Her fears were only amplified when she saw the warrior he was going to face off against.

His opponent was a tall broad-shouldered man that slung a blunt ended mallet around as though it were a feather weight. Sir Almas looked small compared to the giant of a man, and to make matters more nail-biting was that Sir Almas only had a short sword and shield.

The herald of the competition introduced the two men before he raised the white flag up as the two men entered the ring. They walked to the center of the arena and saluted each other before backing away a few paces. Looking down at them, the herald nodded to the two of them before he dropped the flag.

The fight had begun.

The brute of a man circled around the knight as a wolf would do to its prey. Sir Almas got into a fighting stance, facing his attacker and never taking his eyes off of him.

"Ha!" the brute shouted before he stepped toward Sir Almas swinging his mallet like an axe.

Sir Almas spun to the side away from the deadly swings. He spun and took a side swipe at the brute with his sword. Using the handle of his mallet the brute blocked Sir Almas' sword swipe.

Snapping into defensive mode, the knight rapidly backed away from the brute. The brute readjusted his grip on his mallet and pursued the knight with sweeping strides. He made powerful side swings at the knight.

Sir Almas was on a fast retreat around the ring trying to avoid getting bashed in.

When the adversary swung his mallet in a downward motion trying to hit Sir Almas and it struck the ground inches from the knight's feet, the man paused a moment to catch his breath.

Sir Almas saw the opportunity he was looking for.

With lightning fast movements, Sir Almas rose up against the brute. He charged forward with a mighty swing of his sword. The opponent saw the oncoming attack and took a step backward to avoid it, but he did not suspect the knight's underhanded move.

The knight half spun away with his sword and in the same moment swung his shield forward. The shield caught the brute on the side of the face with a nasty right swing. There was a sickening crunch when the shield connected with the side of the brute's face.

Unprotected and unprepared, the knight took the full brunt of the attack.

Dazed the brute recoiled back a few stumbling steps. Straightening up unsteadily, his weapon slipped from his grasp as he let out a low groan before his eyes rolled back and he toppled backward onto the ground.

The brute laid before Sir Almas knocked out cold.

"Champion!" the herald declared jumping down into the ring and walked over to Sir Almas; taking ahold of his arm he raised his hand high in the air.

"Win one for Oak Land, their champion, Sir Almas Martin!"

Cheers rose from the crowd of spectators that were squeezed in close to watch the match.

Raising the sword in his other hand in the air, Sir Almas stood in the center of the ring soaking up the glory of the moment.

Della was glad and relieved that he had won, but she found herself feeling disgusted by the events she had just witnessed.

Now she understood why Amelia hated the games so much.

Chapter

23

"How much more fighting do you have to do?" Della asked Sir Almas after they returned to the tent.

She held onto the knight's helmet as he washed the dirt and sweat off his face and out of his hair.

"Hopefully only two more ground combat fights," he replied. "If all goes well, then I will have an easy day."

"I see," Della said nodding.

"Are you hungry?" he asked her as he dried his face off.

"Only if you are," Della said looking down at the ground.

"Why do you do that?" Sir Almas asked pausing to look at her.

"Do what?"

"Look down when I am speaking to you. Della, I am not your master, you don't need to keep doing that."

"Sorry…it's just a habit." Della whispered.

"Well, you must learn to forget the past. You are a free woman now and that means you have a chance to start over, to build a new life."

Della did not speak, but only nodded.

How can I when I don't know how? Where do I even begin? her thoughts swirled around in her head like mad.

"Never mind all of that for now." Sir Almas said with a dismissive wave of his hand.

"Come now, let's go find something to eat."

Taking his helmet from her, he tucked it underneath his arm before he led the way through the camp out toward the market area. He brought her to a quaint little corner market booth near the front gate of the castle.

A short thin man, with wiry grey hair, and wearing a dark green hooded robe cooked over an open firepit. He had a small counter on which to serve his customers and four stools for them to sit on.

"How may I help ye?" he inquired in a high-pitched tone.

The robed man turned away from the pan of steaks he had cooking over the open fire to face his new customers. He had a narrow face, pale complexion, and a thin greyish-black long greasy beard. He had small green eyes set deep into his hallowed eye sockets; his features were mysterious and friendly all at once.

"We are looking for something to fill ourselves up on and something refreshing to drink." Sir Almas announced while offering Della a seat.

"Can ye pay?" the man asked. "I don't take promises or trades."

"Yes, I can." the knight replied pulling a few coppers from his coin pouch and tossed it on the counter between them.

The merchant nodded his head, seemingly pleased with what he had been given.

"Well, I have a little roast rabbit left, swine, and fried fish. I still got a little venison, but it'll cost extra because it's difficult to come by." the merchant listed as he pulled up two jugs from underneath the table and set them before Sir Almas and Della.

"Got water and mead for you."

"All right," Sir Almas acknowledged with a pleased nod. "Della, what would you like?"

Della stood there marveling at all the choices of meat to eat, Sir Almas knew that all the choices must have felt overwhelming.

"Some fish," Della muttered in her usual low tone.

"Excellent choice." Sir Almas approved.

"Two servings of fish and some mead if you will." Sir Almas ordered tapping his knuckle on the countertop.

Quickly, the merchant collected the coinage before he went on to make their meal. First, he brought two clay cups over and filled them before setting two tin plates out in front of them. When he was done with this, he pulled two fish out of a basket and started to work preparing them for frying.

"While we are waiting, you can tell me a little about you." the knight requested turning his full attention toward her.

Della swallowed hard and paled when she heard the knight's request. Being asked this made Della want to run and hide somewhere.

Why does he want to know about me? For what reason? she thought in panicked fear.

"Come now, I won't hurt you." he promised her.

Della's words froze in her throat and try as she might, she could not respond.

"Okay, how about we try something a little different," Sir Almas suggested thoughtfully.

"I'll tell you one thing about me and in return you can tell me something about you."

Della did not know how to answer, she just sat there and stared at the knight with uncertainty.

"Let's see…well, I have been in service to the kingdom of Oak Land for a little over fifteen years."

"Now it's your turn."

Della still hesitated, nervously rubbing a hand across her knee.

"Don't worry, whatever you choose to tell me, I vow not to repeat it. Your secrets are safe with me." he assured her.

Della gave it more thought before she figured out how she could respond.

"Um, I come from the kingdom of Millet in the land of Varamor." she answered scarcely above a whisper.

"See that wasn't so bad." Sir Almas declared approvingly.

"Okay, next one. My mother was from the kingdom of Hitterdal Land."

"I had a grandmother on my father's side." Della said.

"Ah, I see," the knight acknowledged his face becoming grave.

"Our parents, Amelia and mine, they..." Sir Almas paused clearing his throat.

"They died during the Keltar Nor Wars. Our mother died when a terrible fire swept through our area of the city during the first assault on the city by Sand Land during the Keltar Nor Wars. Over two hundred people perished in that fire and it was almost the breaking point for Oak Land in its fight against the invading kingdom of Sand Land.

Shortly after the fire, though, the kingdom of Delmar came to our aid and with the leadership of our father we were able to defeat the kingdom of Sand Land, but it cost our father his life."

Della's heart ached for the knight understanding the pain he was suffering through. She felt immense pity for him.

"My parents died when I was young too," Della spoke up. "A plague swept through our kingdom and they died quickly. I was left in the care of my grandmother."

Sir Almas shared a look of sympathy with her.

"She..." Della's voice broke as she thought back to those terrible early years. "She was the one who—who sold me into the slave trade."

A look of utter shock and horror came over Sir Almas' face as this was revealed to him.

"Oh, no!" he gasped.

"She was the reason I was put into the horrible trade. I would not have been in this mess if it weren't for her." Della said bitterly.

"And you still harbor anger for her?" Sir Almas asked.

"She destroyed everything!" Della said in resentment.

"Does she still live?"

"I don't know. Probably not, she drank far too much." Della said carelessly.

"Then what good does it do you being angry at her? If she is dead, why stay so mad?"

"Because I hate her memory!" Della snapped.

"It's not right, Della, not good." he gently scolded. "Jesus teaches us forgiveness. He even forgives the most grievous betrayals and sins. We must learn to do as He does, even though it will be difficult."

"Never! I will never forgive that woman!" Della countered sternly as she turned away.

"Della, please," Sir Almas pleaded in frustration. "Don't shut me out."

"I want to help you. To help teach you forgiveness and to find peaceful happiness."

Della did not turn around; she turned her face upward trying to hold back the tears that were welling in her eyes.

"Della?" the knight tried again.

When Della didn't respond; Sir Almas reluctantly let all conversation drop. He hated giving up on speaking to the young woman, especially when she was just beginning to open up about her past.

But anger ruled her life and overpowered any chance of him finding out about her past or reasoning with her.

Oh, Lord, I need Your help. Sir Almas prayed earnestly. *I know I can't get through to Della alone. You are the only One who can show her the way to learning to let her anger go. To show her the true path to forgiveness and healing.*

Sir Almas sighed deeply, feeling defeat creep up on him. He knew when he felt this way, he had to put all his faith and trust in God to handle things.

Chapter
24

Sir Almas had successfully won his combat sets and stood at the top tier of the rankings for the title of champion. Jousting was the next looming challenge before the knight and the remaining competition was tougher.

The day when Sir Almas was set to compete; Amelia decided to come along to watch, joining Della and Priest Lumis in the seating area.

The arena was long and rectangular with two alley ways for the jousting competitors to ride down and between them was a railing partition. On one side of the arena that was upraised and had comfortable cushioned seating and canopy's overhead was where the noblemen and their families sat.

On the opposite side of the arena was the seating area for the wealthy and commoners. The seating were three hardwood benches that were positioned lower than the noblemen's seating arrangements. The poor folks on this side of the arena were not bestowed with a canopy to shade them from the hot rays of the beating sun.

Around the arena railing attached to poles were the flags representing each house in Teary Isles. Unfortunately, at this years' festival, the King of Teary Isles and any knights representing the kingdom of Ravens Burg did not attend.

Sir Almas entered his side of the arena wearing his heavy plate armor and riding his black warhorse Fora.

His competitor was Sir Zulta Blackwell from the kingdom of Wades Worth. Sir Blackwell was the reigning champion of the festival title for two years straight. He was a man of average height, muscularly built, and had long red hair that he wore in a thick braid down his back. He wore all black leather armor, with a grey chest plate, and dark garments. The warhorse he rode was pure white.

The grey steel helmet he wore was carved out to look like a snarling bear and at the end of his lance also was a small bear head. The bear was his family crest, they were the wealthiest family in the kingdom of Wades Worth, owning most of the farmland and a large merchant trade.

The bench was packed with standing room only. Everyone, including the noble family of Oak Land greatly anticipated these jousting tournaments.

Already that day the tournament had been costly, four knights had been severely injured, and one warhorse had perished due to injuries suffered during a match. It was fast in becoming a brutally bloody tournament.

The steward of the match stood near the booth of the Oak Land noble family near an upraised platform. The steward held a white flag up high and waited for the competitors to get in position.

Upon entering the arena, Sir Almas and Sir Blackwell rode their mounts down their alleys at a walk toward each other. When they got close, they lowered their lances so that the tips touched and they saluted each other.

They rode back down to their starting positions and halted while squires made last minute checks and adjustments.

The steward stepped out onto his platform holding the flag tightly; the mounts of the two knights pranced and half-reared in anticipation of what was coming.

Instantly, the flag was dropped.

Sir Blackwell spurred his mount onward; the horse half-reared before galloping powerfully down the alley. Sir Almas cued his mount also charging down toward Sir Blackwell.

Amelia was so nervous and fearful that she buried her face against Captain Toby's shoulder when the charge began. Della was leaning against the railing, gripping it so tightly that her fingers and knuckles were going white.

She was deathly afraid for the knight.

He rode down toward Sir Blackwell with a determined look on his face and flawless form. Within yards of each other they lowered their lances into place and made the final descent. There was a loud bang and crack as wood and metal met, sending wood splintering everywhere.

On impact Sir Almas' lance broke against Sir Blackwell's shield. Sir Blackwell's lance tip glanced off Sir Almas' chest plate and ran up into his exposed shoulder. The impact sent Sir Almas sliding out of the saddle and crashing to the sandy arena flat on his back.

"Almas!" Amelia screamed in horror when she looked up just when Sir Almas was crashing to the ground.

There was a collective sound of gasps and cries from the crowd.

Sir Blackwell rode his mount down to the other end of the lane and turned around. When he flipped the visor of his helmet up, it was easy to see the look of concern on his face.

Sir Almas was laying on his back in the sand, unmoving.

Without giving it a second thought, Della ducked under the railing into the arena and dashed over to where the knight was. She dropped to her knees when she reached Sir Almas' side, she could not tell if he was dead or alive.

Della unbuckled the chin strap on his helmet quickly and pulled it off, tossing it aside.

Sir Almas' eyes fluttered open as he breathed in deeply, his eyes searched randomly until they settled upon her.

Della anxiously gazed into his face.

"Um…ow." the knight moaned slightly shifting his position.

"Are you okay?" Della asked looking the knight over.

She noticed that under his arm where the lance struck, there was a smear of blood and a small crimson patch was growing on the sand under him. She felt her heart catch when she saw the blood.

"He got me good, didn't he?" Sir Almas asked reading her expression.

With tears coming to her eyes, Della only nodded in response.

"Figured as much." the knight grunted tightly. "Amelia is going to kill me…"

Trailing off, Sir Almas' eyes drifted closed.

"Sir Almas?" Della cried out in desperate fear. "N—no! Don't leave!"

Out of frantic panic, she reached for the buckles on his plate armor and began to madly tear at them trying to unfasten them. The tears blurred her vision so that it was difficult to see what she was doing.

"Whoa, whoa, easy there, lass." Priest Lumis reasoned as he quickly interfered.

Reaching out he gently took ahold of her trembling hands and pulled them away from the buckles on the knight's armor, stopping her attempts.

"Don't do that, it could only make things worse." he advised.

His kind watery blue eyes were filled with shared fear and sympathy, as he patiently held onto her wrists.

"He has been grievously wounded; the armor is the only thing holding back any serious bleeding."

Della slowly surrendered her struggles against his restraint and rocked back on her knees sitting down. Letting her wrists go, the Priest moved to the knight as other attendants came up to lend a hand. Soon she was pushed out of the way, as the knight was tended to and carried off the field.

Della was left where she was, feeling like her world was crumbling around her—again.

It felt like just when she was opening up to someone and found a reason to hope, it was being brutally crushed right before her eyes.

Why do dreadful things have to always happen to me? Why to the things I care about must be taken? she pondered sobbing into her hands.

She did not know what she would do if Sir Almas should die.

I will be all alone…again.

Chapter

25

OR THE NEXT TWO NERVE-RACKING DAYS, DELLA PACED THE floor of the house, constantly worrying for Sir Almas. The knight had been brought home and put into his room where Priest Lumis and Sir Blackwell's physician tended to him for hours. Sir Blackwell felt terrible about how the tournament went for Sir Almas and lent his physician in hopes that it would help in some small way.

Finally, by the evening of the first day, Sir Blackwell's physician emerged from the knight's bedroom, exhausted and tense.

There Amelia, and Captain Toby met him.

He informed them the injury Sir Almas had suffered was a severe one and he had a tough time in digging wood splinters from the wound. He warned them that over the next few days it would be touch and go, if Sir Almas could survive the fever and avoid infection settling in, then he would have a good chance of making a full recovery.

For the past two days, the knight had hardly stirred, he was conscious long enough to take a few sips of water. Captain Toby would come by every night he did not have duties, to check in on his friend and offer his fiancée comfort.

Amelia continuously tended to her brother through the day, which rendered her exhausted, and her eyes were blood-shot red from the almost continual crying.

Della had seemingly been overlooked now that Sir Almas was the main concern. She went about the house completely unnoticed by everyone. She was glad for this though, because she wanted to be left alone, but still near the knight. Della was both glad and surprised that they allowed her to be so near Sir Almas.

After all, Amelia and Captain Toby had made it clear that they did not approve of her.

On the afternoon of the third day, Amelia decided to leave the house for a few hours to get a break and visit with Captain Toby's mother who lived next door. When the older woman had gone, immediately Della crept into the knight's bedroom.

The knight somehow looked smaller being tucked underneath the heavy bear skin blanket and a quilt. His raven black hair was matted and sweat drenched; bristles were beginning to grow out on his face. The knight's face was sunken in and his skin was pale from him being as ill as he was.

Della could see the bandage that covered his shoulder, the cloth was wet with sweat and stained with dry blood. The blankets rose and fell ever-so-slightly with Sir Almas' every breath. It scared the young woman more than anything to see the once warm and friendly knight reduced to a sick weakly man on the brink of death. Since the first time she met him, he always appeared so strong and unwavering, she would have never imagined that he could be reduced to this.

As quiet as a mouse and with hesitant strides, Della moved to the knight's bedside. She noticed his hair clung to his forehead from sweating. Lifting her hand, Della reached up and gently stroked the locks of hair from his brow. Sir Almas let out a low moan and moved his head toward the touch of her hand.

Della felt terribly guilty about how she had been treating the knight. When he had given her shelter, care, and a tremendous amount of patience; she gave him nothing in return—not even a thanks.

She had been nothing, but a cruel ungrateful woman, she denied herself the smallest moment of trust. The one person who would never cause her harm nor betray her was lying there at death's door.

"If I should lose you…I." she whispered gazing upon the knight, tears choking of her words.

"Please, please live. I swear I will do anything you want, tell you anything you wish to know. I still need to tell you how much your kindness has meant to me." Della pleaded. "I need to tell you how sorry I am for being such a terrible beast to you!"

I want to tell you so much. she thought tearfully.

I need you to know how much you have come to mean to me.

Della stood next to the knight a while longer before she decided to do something for him. Fetching a bowl of clean water and a soft cloth she came back to his bedside and sat down on the edge of it. Dipping the cloth in the water she began to gently wash the man's face. He still had dirt and sand smudges on his face from three days ago, it appeared cleaning him up was the least of everyone's concerns.

She tended to the knight for several minutes, washing his face, neck, and hands, until she was satisfied with her work. Della had never noticed before how handsome the man was, how there was an ever-present kind expression on his face.

She found that for the first time that she could remember, she was experiencing a feeling she had never felt before. Della oddly felt drawn to the knight and she was starting to feel affection for him. The feeling was so strange that it frightened her, but she refused to push it away. In fact, she found that she really liked this new feeling.

Della lost track of time as she stroked the knight's brow and kept vigil over him.

Suddenly, the front door opened, and the sound of muffled conversation drifted into the house.

Hearing this, Della jumped up off the edge of the bed in startled alarm. She felt that she would be in trouble for going into Sir Almas' room to visit him. Believing that Amelia would yell at her, the young woman rushed out of the room and slipped into the kitchen area before Amelia and Captain Toby came all the way into the house.

"He hasn't spoken yet," Amelia was telling the Captain as they entered the house. "He only wakes up long enough to drink something."

"I know and I worry for him." the Captain reflected anxiously. "He's been injured before during the games—but never this bad."

"I knew him entering the games was a bad idea. I even warned him." Amelia said regretfully.

"I had a bad feeling on the day of the joust—but I never told Almas."

"Why not?" Captain Toby pressed.

"You should have seen him, Toby," Amelia reasoned. "He was so excited, like he was a young man again. Jousting has always been his favorite event and now—now he had someone to watch him compete and take interest.

I just couldn't ruin it for him."

"You mean that girl—the *slave*?" Captain Toby inquired his tone dripping with disfavor.

"Yes, Della, I think that's what my brother said her name was. He took her along with him everywhere he went, showing her around the festival and teaching her about the things he liked."

"I figured his eagerness to compete again might have had something to do with the girl." Captain Toby muttered in dissatisfaction.

"Toby," Amelia's tone became very serious.

"I think this Della girl is more than a charity case for him."

"I know," Captain Toby replied with understanding. "I've known since day one. He was so drawn in by her, she was his special interest."

"That's a first for him…at least since mother and father died. He's never cared for or put his time into anything; to Almas only duty consumed his time and interests."

"You know," Captain Toby paused for a moment. "I can't decide if that is a good or bad thing."

"I know. I can't help, but find it irritating at times. When I try to speak to him about things happening in my life or enjoying conversation over a meal, it is like his mind isn't there. He always has his eyes on that girl…he's so engrossed with her."

"Hmmm." Toby mumbled.

"On duty he has been distracted and when I ask him about it, he confesses that he thinks about the young woman and what her future might hold. In fact, every time we speak it's always about that *woman*, he can't think of anything else."

"I have never seen him so invested in anything the way he is with her." Amelia agreed.

"He has seemed more focused and at peace as of late." Captain Toby remarked thoughtfully.

"As much as I hate to admit it, that woman has been good for him." Amelia grumbled before adding. "He was right all along."

"Almas has always been a well-planned man who can foresee what is to come. That is why he has made such an excellent knight." the Captain noted.

"He didn't see this incident coming." Amelia added bitterly.

"He's not a seer, Amelia." Captain Toby countered gently. "I am only referring to his instincts to make wise choices, most of the time."

"Toby, I am so scared." Amelia relented her voice quivered.

"Now, now," Captain Toby soothed gathering Amelia into his arms. "We must have faith. Almas is in God's caring hands; all we can do now is pray for his recovery."

"I know," Amelia sobbed softly. "I am just so worried about him."

"I am too." Captain Toby confessed as he held Amelia in his arms comforting her.

That evening Priest Lumis returned to check Sir Almas' wounds and inspect his condition. Amelia stood by anxiously as the Priest treated the knight's wound and changed the dressing.

Della finally mustered up enough courage to creep in close to Sir Almas' room, after visiting him earlier and seeing how serious his condition was, she found she couldn't stay away any longer. She stood at the frame of the open door. She watched as the Priest was rubbing salve on the knight's shoulder wound, his gaze moved away from his work and he looked at Della.

"Della," he said gently. "Come forth and help me...please."

Without having to be asked twice, Della entered the room and hurried over to the knight's bedside and stood on the opposite side of the bed from Priest Lumis.

"Take that bandage and begin unraveling it." He instructed as he turn to wash his hands.

Della reached for the bandaged at rested on the knight's chest. When she picked the bandage up, the knight's eyes slowly crept open.

She froze in place when she saw that he was awake. The knight's eyes locked on the ceiling above him for a few moments before his gaze gradually shifted down to her and he smiled weakly.

"D...Della." he muttered in a satisfied whisper.

Chapter

26

Upon Sir Almas waking up, Amelia rushed out of the house and went next door to get Captain Toby to tell him the good news. Priest Lumis asked the knight a list of questions as he took the bandage from Della and continued to tend to him.

When Amelia and the Captain returned, Della quietly slipped off the bed and out of the room allowing the group to enjoy their time of relief and excitement. Knowing that Sir Almas had not eaten in days, the young woman set to work preparing him something to eat.

Going into the kitchen, she got onions, water, and herbs. Stoking up a blazing fire, she put the kettle on. She cut the onions up and sprinkled the soup with herbs until she was satisfied with the flavor. It payed off to have been part of the staff in the royal kitchens of a kingdom because she learned how to cook well.

Once the broth was finished, Della filled a wooden bowl with it, grabbed a spoon and carried it over to Sir Almas's room.

The knight was still wide awake and was now in a sitting position with his back propped up by pillows, listening to Amelia as she told him all about the happenings in the days that he had been sick with fever.

Della stopped in the threshold of the room, suddenly feeling unsure of herself.

What am I doing? she asked herself as she felt fear creep up on her.

"Ah, what a fine smelling dish." Priest Lumis announced sniffing.

He turned away from his satchel of belongings and looked over at Della, who was standing stock still and unsure at the door of the room.

"Good, you have brought the next best thing for Almas." the Priest declared smiling with approval. "Come, bring it over, child."

Sir Almas looked at her and smiled his warm welcoming smile. Captain Toby and Amelia's attention was drawn over to the young woman. Della did not like to be the center of attention, but she focused on Sir Almas and walked slowly over to him carrying the soup.

"Well, I think I could get used to being treated like a king." Sir Almas remarked smiling broadly.

"Don't get too comfortable," Captain Toby jested. "I will whip you into shape as soon as you're back on your feet."

"Of course, task master." Sir Almas joked back.

Everyone around the room laughed at this.

"Ouch," Sir Almas groaned rubbing his sore shoulder. "Laughing is painful."

"It should be." Priest Lumis remarked. "You've paid a high price for a moment of glory."

At this, Sir Almas's expression changed to a grim frown. Noticing the mood change between the two men, Amelia became at once concerned.

"What do you mean?" she asked.

"Ask your brother." the Priest replied motioning to the bedridden knight.

"Almas, what does Priest Lumis mean?" his sister's tone was edged with worry.

"It's—ah," Sir Almas stammered looking down at his hand that rested in his lap. "It's not something we need to talk about right now."

"Almas, if it's serious, you need to tell me now." Amelia pressed.

"It's not, Amelia." Sir Almas quickly countered.

"It's not serious, don't worry we can talk about it later."

"Almas," Amelia began to plead, but her brother shot her a firm dismissive glare.

"Not now." he uttered under his breath.

The room was engulfed in heavy silence, until Priest Lumis spoke up.

"Well, I must be off, there are more who need my healing herbs." he announced picking up his satchel and headed for the door.

"I will walk you out," Captain Toby offered as he nodded to Amelia.

"Yes…we will." she confirmed catching the Captain's hint.

"By the way," Priest Lumis said half-turning back to look at Sir Almas.

"Remember to take it easy for a few weeks. You don't want to prolong your injury."

"No, sir, I don't." Sir Almas agreed nodding.

"Thank you, again, Tal."

Priest Lumis bowed his head solemnly and left the room followed closely by Captain Toby and Amelia. Once they had left the room, Sir Almas turned his attention to Della who was standing beside his bed cradling the bowl of soup.

"Della, thank you for bringing me something to eat." Sir Almas said gratefully.

Della gave the bowl to the knight, before she climbed up on the edge of the bed. Sir Almas took the bowl in his good hand and rested it on his chest just under his chin. Taking the spoon, Della dipped it into the warm broth and brought it to the knight's lips.

"M-m-m-m, that's good." Sir Almas muttered with delight. "Wow, I never thought broth could be so delicious."

Della ducked her head and blushed as a little smile came to her lips. She slowly and patiently fed the knight the broth and used a towel to wipe his chin and beard.

"You know," he said as Della set the empty bowl aside.

"Twice I have been blessed enough to have an angel to look after me. Once when I was lying in the arena and here when I woke."

Della's headed snapped up in surprise, and her face turned a shade of red with embarrassment.

"God has been good to me." he said settling back against the pillows and closed his eyes.

"He sent me an angel..."

Della sat there in silence unsure of how to react to what he told her. No one had ever called her something like that before.

An angel? she thought in disbelief.

He must care a great deal for me...perhaps more than anyone knows.

Della was almost afraid of this new, strange feeling. She was beginning to feel an attraction toward the knight—a feeling she had never known before.

What should I do? she pondered. *Should I embrace or deny what I am feeling for him?*

For the next few days, Della tended to Sir Almas by cooking meals for him and sitting at his bedside letting him speak to her. Sir Almas would converse with her for hours; talking about his everyday life before she came, growing up with Amelia, and he described in detail about the kingdoms and people of Teary Isles.

In turn, Della would tell him what little she remembered of her parents and home kingdom, her time as a castle kitchen maid, and about her country. She still had not told him about her years as a camp slave, she just was not ready to go that far yet.

She noticed something about the knight that was concerning to her.

The was a change in the knight's attitude, his mood was somehow different. He did not seem so bright, encouraging, and positive like he used to be. Something had changed in him; he had his mind on something.

One day, Della found out what it was.

It was a warm sunny afternoon when Della came into the knight's room with his usual noon meal. Sir Almas was lying looking toward the open window where the shafts of warm sunlight shone on his face.

Della observed that he had a forlorn expression on his face and his eyes were grave. When he heard her shoes scrape against the stone floor, he glanced over in her direction. This time, he did not greet her or smile as he had done in the past, instead his eyes were filled with great sadness.

"I can't deny it any longer, Della." he said mournfully. "I can't run from the truth—the reality that stares me in the face."

Della came around to the side of the bed and set the tray on the stand near his headboard. Then she sat down on the edge of the bed and gave him her full attention.

"Do you recall when Priest Lumis said I paid a high price for a moment of glory?" he asked her.

Della nodded.

"Well, he wasn't wrong." Sir Almas sighed deeply.

Della gave him a puzzled look.

"For all my troubles…for refusing to heed all the pleads and warnings from my friends and family; I went ahead and did it anyways," Sir Almas grumbled with despairing in his tone.

"Like a fool I jousted and now, my arm is permanently damaged."

Sir Almas winced as he slightly raised it up from where it rested in his lap to show Della. He was only able to flex his thumb and middle finger.

"I never will be able to use it properly again." as he said this, tears welled in his eyes.

"My time as a knight is over," he said bitterly.

"I cannot use my left arm—my sword arm. I will not be able to properly exercise my duty as a knight of Oak Land."

Seeing the loss and desolation in the knight's eyes was

heartbreaking. She understood that the knight was losing one of the most important things in his life, and there was nothing she could do to help him.

"What am I if I can't be a knight?" he whispered hoarsely as he hung his head.

Della did not know what to say or do, it was pure torture for her to watch the knight's world shattering before him.

"I haven't told anyone," he spoke slowly. "Only you and Priest Lumis know. Because…I thought there was some way around it, and I was hoping that it wasn't permanent or that the damage would only be minor."

Della only sat beside the knight in silence, but she gave him her full attention.

"I still don't know how—how I will break it to Amelia." he said numbly.

"Must you?" Della asked.

Sir Almas shot her a puzzled look of surprise.

"I am not sure what you mean."

"Do you have to tell your sister the truth right now?" Della proposed. "Perhaps there is still a chance of your arm healing more fully and you can go back to your duties."

"No, Priest Lumis informed me that there is no going back. The damage is done." the knight replied frowning.

"Then you are just going to give up?"

"What else is there left for me to do?"

"Keep trying to work it, you can't just give up before you have even started trying."

"Don't you think I have thought of that already?" Sir Almas countered sharply. "I have been trying, Della. When no one is around, I have tried to force myself to move and flex my hand. It doesn't work, I—I can't do it."

"It's too soon," Della reasoned patiently. "Your accident only happened a few short weeks ago. If you keep forcing movement, your arm will never heal properly."

"No, it's over Della. I know I will never be able to properly use it again," the knight insisted bitterly. "I should have noticed some kind of a change by now, but nothing has happened."

"You can't just quit!" Della pleaded.

"My time as a knight is over and I will just have to start making a living doing something else." Sir Almas said with a hopeless look in his eyes. "There is no other way."

"No, you have to keep trying," the young woman resisted. "Just like you did with me, when I was being nothing, but difficult and everyone kept telling you I was a lost cause. You never gave up on me and now look at where we are."

"That was different, Della, there was truly hope," Sir Almas pointed out. "My arm is useless; you can see it just as clearly as I can."

It was too much for Della to sit there and listen to the knight give up on what he loved and pursued wholeheartedly.

"Perhaps, I can try my hand at being a farmer." Sir Almas pondered, with little enthusiasm.

Hearing him utter this was soul crushing for Della.

Not wanting to see the sorrow on Sir Almas' face nor the tears welling in his eyes; Della quickly rose from the edge of the bed and rushed out of the room. She ran through the main room and burst out the front door.

Della kept running, through the streets and out the main gate until she found herself out near an open field of golden barley. She knelt at the edge of the field, burying her face in her hands she began to sob. It was the worst feeling in the world to see the man who fought to make her want to live, now crumbling without hope.

Being a knight was Sir Almas's life—without it he was a man without hope, half the man he now was.

Part 2

Be kind to one another, tenderhearted, forgiving one another, as God in Christ forgave you.'

EPHESIANS 4:32

Chapter
27

A CLOAK OF HEAVY GLOOM ENVELOPED THE MARTIN home. Amelia spent much of her time either out with Captain Toby or over at his mother's home planning their soon-to-be wedding, with her friends. Amelia and Captain Toby decided to delay their wedding until winter or spring, mostly due to Sir Almas's condition.

Sir Almas was able to get out of bed and around enough to go from his bed to the main room of the house and would often sit on his chair out in front of the house. The knight hardly spoke or smiled anymore.

It was as if giving up on being a knight, had taken the life out of Sir Almas, robbing him of his joy and peace.

These days, Della felt compelled to stay near Sir Almas, she figured that since she was a stranger in a strange land and had nowhere to go, he was her only provider of safe refuge. The knight would often sit on his wicker chair out in front of the house and stare off blankly for hours on end.

Often, Della would busy herself with household chores and sewing, but she was sure she stayed nearby so she could hear if the knight called to her. The knight continued with his troublesome routine for over a month and no one was able to console him out of it.

At wits end, Della decided to seek out an innovative approach to helping the knight change his attitude toward his current situation. She figured that Sir Almas could never properly use his left arm, but what about retraining himself to use his right hand?

Curious about this, and whether it would work or not, she sought out the advice of Priest Lumis.

"Well, it's entirely possible," Priest Lumis said thoughtfully as he rummaged among his things.

"There is nothing wrong with his right arm whatsoever."

Della had been able to sneak out of the house one afternoon while Amelia and Captain Toby came to Sir Almas with a list of wedding plans, they wished to share with him. After getting directions to the Priest's home from the Captain, Della went on her way, but told no one what she was up to.

Priest Lumis was delighted to have her over and put on a kettle of tea after he invited her into his sitting room.

Priest Lumis finally found the tonic bottle he was searching for before he went over and sat down at his desk chair once more.

"Please, have a slice of raisin bread." he offered nodding to the plate laid out on his desk near where the young woman sat.

"No, thanks." Della politely refused.

"How's your tea, dear?" he asked with care.

"It's good," Della said giving a slight smile.

"You know," Priest Lumis began as he folded his hand on the desk in front of him and look directly at Della.

"You have been the only person who has come to me asking how you can help Sir Almas. I am wondering why that is. What does his wellbeing matter to you?"

"Sir Almas has been ever so kind to me, and I can't bear to see him this way." Della explained with nervous hesitation.

"From what Sir Almas has told me about you, it seems like you don't really trust anyone. So, how is it you can care about Sir Almas, if you don't trust him?"

Della was beginning to feel uncomfortable; she did not like being questioned.

It made her feel like she was being accused of a crime.

"As I have said before, he has been kind to me and has given me a place to stay. Instead of sending me away with the other women that were rescued, like everyone was telling him to."

"Why do you think he did that?"

"I…I don't know."

"You know what I think," Priest Lumis muttered while he mixed the tonic with another bottle of liquid.

"I think he did it because he cared about you out of love."

Della was not sure where Priest Lumis was going with his questions, but she got an uneasy feeling from the topic he was discussing.

"I also believe that if anyone can help Sir Almas, that person is you. He most likely won't listen to anyone, but you."

"He will listen to Amelia." Della interceded.

"He didn't stop participating in the festival games, even though Amelia had been begging for him to quit for the past several years." Priest Lumis pointed out.

"No, this is a delicate topic for Sir Almas, and he needs someone outside of his family to challenge him on it."

"I have tried to speak to him about is injury before, but he wouldn't really listen to me." Della replied.

"Then don't be afraid to get firm with him if you must." Priest Lumis encouraged. "Don't allow him to bully you into silence or shut you out. Push him to the limits."

"How? I am only a guest in his house, he could just throw me out if he wants to."

"He won't. He cares too much about you."

"It's not my place."

"Not your place?" the Priest gave her an astonished look.

"If you care at all for Sir Almas, then it is more than your place to try and help him. Everyone in Sir Almas' life is either too scared or resigned. They will not challenge him or his decision, because they do not wish to upset him.

But I say that you will be doing him a worse disservice by not saying something or trying to help him in any way you can. If no one helps Sir Almas, then his life will be and unhappily filled with bleak hopelessness.

Knighthood gives him purpose!" Priest Lumis said passionately.

"I...I don't know if I can." Della stammered.

"I strongly believe that you can," Priest Lumis countered firmly. "Have faith, child!"

"God put you in that man's life for a reason—and perhaps this is that very reason!

It'll be hard at times and it may even feel like a defeating purpose, but if you stay persistent the reward in the end will be more than worth it."

"I'll try my best," Della relented still feeling doubtful.

"I know you will," the Priest said giving her a reassuring nod. "With the Lord's guidance and blessings, you will go far. Remember to just come to me should you have any questions or need help."

Della nodded and gave Priest Lumis a smile and bow of her head as thanks.

"Oh, and Della." Priest Lumis noted giving her a serious look.

"The road to recovery for Sir Almas will be exceedingly difficult and trying for you both. Be strong and never give up."

Chapter

28

ELLA DECIDED TO USE HER BEST STRATEGY FIRST; TO get Sir Almas to take her for walks and to show her around her new home. As usual by noon, Sir Almas had eaten breakfast and went out to sit in his wicker chair out in front of the house.

Amelia had left with Captain Toby's mother to buy cooking goods and would be absent for most of the day. Della hurried to clear the table of dirty dishes and tidied up around the house so she could go out for a walk with Sir Almas as soon as possible.

As soon as she was done with her daily tasks, Della packed a small parcel of food and grabbed a jug of water. She took up the walking stick Priest Lumis gave to her for Sir Almas to use. The walking stick was for the knight to lean on with his good hand to help keep him steady for he had not fully recovered his strength.

When Della emerged from the front door, Sir Almas looked in her direction and gave her a strange look.

"What's this?" he asked faintly smiling.

"I want to go for a walk." Della said.

"Really? Where to?" the knight asked looking amused.

"Well, I was hoping you could help me with that." she countered smiling eagerly.

"Hmm, how so?"

"I want to see more of the kingdom of Oak Land." Della replied.

"I have seen much of the city, but I want to see the countryside outside of the castle wall."

"Why?"

"It's my home now, and I want to get to better know where I live." Della inquired innocently.

"Okay," Sir Almas acknowledge nodding slowly.

"Will you take me?" Della inquired innocently.

"I don't know," Sir Almas said frowning uncomfortably. "I don't feel much like going anywhere."

"Please? I don't know my way around Oak Land, and I could get lost without the proper guidance."

"No, I really can't." he said shaking his head.

"Please, just this once." Della pressed earnestly.

"I...I don't know if—"

"I have this for you," Della declared presenting the walking stick to the knight.

"Oh," he said with a look of surprise. "So, I am to be like an old man, a cripple."

Della felt awkward by the knight's comment, she felt ashamed of bringing the staff to Sir Almas after he made his remark.

"I am sorry, I didn't mean..."

"Never mind," Sir Almas said dismissively, seeing the look of disappointment on the young woman's face.

He stiffly rose from his seat and accepted the staff from Della.

"All right, let's go." he urged nodding her onward.

Willingly, Della started forward, but kept her pace even with the knight's. He said nothing as they passed through the alleys and streets. When they got to the gate, the guard standing present gave them a nod and smile letting them pass.

"Why don't we head north," Sir Almas suggested leading on the left side of the trail.

A few farmers and villagers passed along the countryside going about their daily duties and normal routines. The harvest was just beginning, and a group of threshers and gathers were working in a nearby barley field. Della liked it there, it was so peaceful and quiet out in the country. The people, though private, were kind and friendly enough.

Della's joys were dampened when she looked at the knight and realized that he was not smiling and still held an expression of gloom on his face. His mood was making Della feel sorrowful.

Is the old Sir Almas gone? Has he truly given up? she wondered as a feeling of defeat came over her.

Sir Almas and she hiked well over two miles away from the main gate of the castle. He had taken her down a winding trail that led between two fields of wheat and through a small grove of trees. The path came to an end at a clearing surrounded by pine and oak trees. At the center of the clearing was a beautiful little pond, with fair-sized boulders near the water's edge.

The clearing was warm and gorgeous.

"A perfect spot for a little break." Sir Almas suggested pausing at the edge of the clearing, allowing Della to take in the beauty of the place for a moment.

"Yes." Della said with a satisfied tone.

"Let's go sit by the pond." Sir Almas said starting over to it.

When they reached the pond, Sir Almas took a seat upon a flat-topped boulder. Della opened the parcel she was carrying and pulled out a half a loaf of dill bread wrapped in a cloth out along with a little square of cheese.

Della had also packed two medium sized apples, that she pulled out and set aside for later. Sir Almas pulled his dagger from the sheath and began to slice the bread. For a while the knight stared at the loaf of bread, he held in his good hand, his expression was of frustration.

Immediately, Della saw what the difficulty was, she almost reached out to take the bread from the knight to cut it herself.

She stopped short.

"Here," she offered giving the knight a sharp knife and traded for the bread. "You cut and I'll hold."

Without a word, the knight did as she suggested. With her help, they had two sandwiches made in no time at all.

"Della," Sir Almas began thoughtfully as he took his bread and cheese.

The young woman looked up at the knight, seeing that his expression had changed becoming very somber.

"I know what you are trying to do," he said taking a bite. "It won't work. I have made my decision."

"Must you decide so soon?" Della questioned, knowing it would be wrong to deny the truth.

"Yes, because I have learned to accept reality and live with it."

"No, you're just quitting."

"What else can I do?" Sir Almas countered throwing his free hand up in frustration.

"I cannot use this hand properly, my sword hand. Without my sword hand, I cannot execute my position as a knight."

"What about your left hand?" Della challenged. "Can't you retrain yourself to use that hand?"

"It would take far too much time…which I don't have." Sir Almas reasoned.

"Why don't you have enough time?" Della countered.

"Captain Toby won't be able to hold my position open forever. A decision will have to be made sooner or later, presumably before winter." he informed her. "I know that I will not be able to use my right hand properly by that time."

"Not so very long ago I thought I was doomed to a life of entertainment for the army of Millet for the remainder of my life. I had no hope of doing anything else—or escaping it." Della said haltingly.

"Then when I was ready to end it all—to give up, a certain person came into my life and changed all of that. For months I have been wondering why he helped me, why he saved me, why he protected me despite what all his friends were telling him.

Then one day it struck me, he saw something in me, perhaps he saw a glimmer of hope. He believed that I could change, that I could be a better happier person and he wasn't wrong."

Della looked into the knight's eyes.

"And for the first time since I was a little girl I have dared to dream. Something I never thought I would do again."

Sir Almas gave her a solemn look of appreciation and surprise.

"I don't know if I can do it," Sir Almas confessed lowering his gaze. "This—has set me back Della, I wasn't ready for it."

"You don't have to worry, because you won't do this alone." Della assured him. "I am going to help you every step of the way, no matter how hard it will be or how long it takes. I want to help you make a comeback—don't let this handicap become you."

"Are you certain about this… it could be a long-term commitment." Sir Almas asked hesitantly.

"Of course, I am." Della said firmly. "Where else would I go? Besides, you have helped me and now it's only fair that I return the favor."

"All right," Sir Almas replied with lingering uncertainty.

"We can try it your way."

"Good," Della said nodding in approval.

"Come let us eat, we don't want to be away too long, or Amelia will start worrying." Sir Almas pointed out.

They began their journey home a half hour later. On their way back to the castle, they came to a patch of wildflowers. Sir Almas veered off the trail and stepped into the abundantly blooming patch.

"Look, it's daisies and lilies." he remarked gesturing to the beautiful flowers.

"Amelia loves lilies."

For the first time since the accident a smile spread across Sir Almas's face and a sparkle came into his eyes.

"I think I'll surprise her by bringing some home."

Sir Almas picked daisies and lilies, making a small fistful. Finding a beautiful baby's breath; the knight plucked it up and turned to Della, offering it to her. Speechlessly, Della accepted it and Sir Almas gave her a warm smile as their fingers brushed against each other.

Della could not help feeling a burst of joy and felt herself blush.

She began to wonder if their relationship was growing into more than just a friendship.

Can he be falling in love with me…just as I have for him? Della's mind ran over all the possibilities.

Chapter

29

ELLA MADE SURE SHE PRESERVED THE FLOWER WHEN she got home by placing it between the pages of one of the parchment books in her room. It was the first gift she had received since her parents were alive. Even though it was only a flower, to Della the gift meant the world to her.

Before the sun rose the following morning, Sir Almas was up and busy preparing the morning meal in the kitchen. Della dressed in her old comfortable clothes, she like the feel of the leather. Della knew that most of the people within Oak Land would not approve, but she felt that the knight would not mind. Della pulled her hair back into a loose braid before she headed into the kitchen area.

Sir Almas had made biscuits and warmed the leftover chicken from the evening before, along with a bowl of fresh fruit and a glass of cider on the side.

"Oh, good morning Della." he greeted when he spotted her.

"Good morning," Della humbly greeted.

The knight struggled with the two plates as he tried to carry them over to the table.

"Here," Della said as she quickly hurried over and took one of the plates from the knight. "Let me help."

"Thanks." Sir Almas said in a grateful tone.

"Won't Amelia be joining us?" Della inquired noticing only two places set out.

"No," the knight replied looking down for a moment.

"She went out with some of her friends—she'll be out for most of the day."

"Oh," Della acknowledged with a solemn nod.

"Well, have a seat." Sir Almas invited motioning to the empty seat across the table from him.

Della took note of the unusually rich breakfast; normally they would have bread, and cheese or just some porridge.

She noticed how tense and distracted Sir Almas seemed. Silently, he brought two glasses of cider in and set them out before he took his seat.

"You have dressed in your old clothes again." Sir Almas noted nodding at her outfit.

The knight didn't mind how she chose to dress, he felt that if she was comfortable in her old clothes it was all that mattered, which was more important than what society thought. Still, he knew how judgmental and cruel the people in his kingdom could be.

Della's bare arms and from just above her knees down, and waistline to ribs showed. She had changed the top, instead of the neckline plunging down, she sewed a dark linen material to cover more of her bare chest.

To many, though, she would seem practically naked.

It is the customary dress of her people—but my people will never understand. he reflected with pity. *Will she be able to put up with the ridicule and judgement?*

"Y—yes," Della said quietly. "I…like it."

"It looks good on you." Sir Almas commented with an approving nod.

Della ducked her head.

"Let's pray," the knight suggested.

He offered Della his good hand, Della hesitated uncertainly for a second or two before she took ahold of his hand.

"Dear Lord, we thank You for this abundance of nourishing food You have blessed us with. Help us to conduct ourselves well today. Amen." the knight prayed.

Della slowly opened her eyes after a moment, her hand lingered in the gentle grasp of the knight. Suddenly, the knight took notice that they were holding hands, quickly, he drew his away and a look of embarrassment came over his face.

"I…I am sorry." he apologized bashfully.

"No mind." Della replied taking up her fork.

It was true, she had not minded one bit that the knight held onto her hand. It was the kindest gesture she had experienced for some time. When he held her hand in his; she felt warm and bubbly.

Does he feel the same? she wondered watching him put honey on a biscuit.

Sir Almas fought hard to keep his focus on the task at hand to keep from staring at the young woman across from him.

Della would take offense to me staring at her like a fool. the knight figured.

He found it a struggle not to look at Della; her beauty was so breath-taking, it was something he had known since day one, but tried to ignore it. Giving it a little thought, he realized why he had not noticed her natural beauty for so long.

She had been dressed like an Oak Lander for the past several weeks, in long sleeve dresses, high collars and skirts to her ankles. Her hair had been hidden underneath the cover of a scarf most of the time. Being dressed as an Oak Lander was not for Della; it masked too much of her beauty.

She was truly a Varamorean—a beautiful woman.

Something is happening to me. Sir Almas thought making the stark connection.

His eyes travelled up from his plate and met with the gaze of the young woman and it was at that moment; he knew the feelings were real.

I believe I am falling in love!

"What is the plan for today?" Della asked as Sir Almas walked with her out to the pond in the clearing.

She noticed that the knight carried a pack over his good shoulder that was heavily weighed down. He also had his sword strapped to his waist—something he had not done since before his accident.

"You shall see." he replied vaguely as he strode onward, his face was bright and there was a look in his eyes that had been missing since before the accident.

It was hope.

He acted more like his old positive self, though his face was still pale and drawn, and he favored his injured arm.

Della was happy all the same; it was the first signs of improvement.

Chapter

30

"OKAY, I BROUGHT THIS RAWHIDE ROPE WITH US—
because I need your help to use it." Sir Almas
explained pulling a long-braided rope from the pack
and two metal weighting blocks.

Della picked one of the blocks up and found it was rather heavy.

"Those are for later." he said dismissively taking the weight out
of her hand and set it aside.

"First, we do this." he said holding the rope up.

"I need you to grab this end and I'll hold onto the other."

Della took the end of the rope and gave him a very perplexed
look.

"Hold on tight," he instructed. "I'll pull on my end until your
arm is extended tautly towards me and then you in turn will do the
same."

"Got it?"

"Yes, I believe so." she replied nodding thoughtfully.

"I don't want you to stop or hold back—no matter how much pain it causes me. I want to strengthen this arm, okay?" he said motioning to his injured arm.

"Pull hard."

"I understand." Della said not liking the challenge she was facing.

The last thing she ever wanted to do was to cause the knight any sort of pain.

"Ready?" Sir Almas asked wrapping the rope around the palm of his formerly injured arm and winced as he tugged on it to make sure it was tight.

Della nodded.

Sir Almas clenched his teeth as his eyes glazed over from the rush of pain when he closed his hand into a fist. He slowly, but firmly pulled the rope to him and gave it a finishing tug. The action caused Della to clumsily step forward two steps before she was able to stop herself.

Della hesitated for only a moment before she brought the rope back to her and pulled hard until it stopped.

The rough jolting pull made Sir Almas grunt with pain, but he held on tight to his end. He looked at her with firm determination and gave a nod to continue. By the twentieth pull, Della could tell that the knight was struggling.

Della wanted to stop, but she feared upsetting the knight and causing him to snap at her.

The knight managed two more pulls before his injured arm began to shake too violently for him to continue. His arm was too weak and part ways through pulling the rope back towards him, his arm gave away under the strain.

"Augh!" the knight exclaimed in annoyed frustration.

The knight cursed in anger under his breath, picking up the rope in his good hand he yanked it out of Della's hands. Taking the rope, he tossed it away.

Della stood before the knight, frozen in petrified fear.

"It's no use!" Sir Almas exclaimed in exasperation.

"It's too early." Della quickly objected. "This is only your first try."

"Yes, and I can't even hardly pull a rope with minor resistance." the knight growled pointing to the cast away braided rope.

"You are pushing yourself too hard." the young woman stubbornly argued.

"I have to if I want to keep my position as a knight of Oak Land."

Della felt slightly afraid of the knight when he was in such a mood, but she recalled what Priest Lumis had told her about helping the knight.

"I know," Della's voice faded to almost a whisper.

"But you must be patient. These things will take time. You won't get better instantly; you cannot force results."

"When did you become such a philosopher?" Sir Almas remarked with a bitter air.

For a long moment, Della was humbly and obediently silenced by the knight's harsh remark. Then something rose in her that she had long ago buried; and his words angered her more than they offended.

"Do you want to return to duty or not!" she shouted.

Sir Almas's head shot up and he stared at her in startled surprise.

"I am tired of you feeling sorry for yourself all the time. Either you let me help you or I will leave you to do whatever you please! You can even choose to give up—if you wish."

Della's outburst caught Sir Almas off guard; he had become to accustomed to her being so soft spoken that he never expected her to shout at him.

"I want to see you get better, but you don't seem to want to try!" Della continued frowning deeply in sorrowful frustration.

"I—I don't think I can continue on like this anymore and face the disappointment—I want the old Almas back.

The one that pushed me to become a better person, to explore my new home. The one who convinced me not to run away, when it was the only thing that made sense at the time."

Sir Almas could see the deep emotion on Della's face; tears welled in her eyes as she stared into his.

"I took a chance and stayed because…you said you really cared about me." Della said lowering her gaze to the ground.

Della's words struck Sir Almas to the heart; every word of it, he knew was more than true.

As much as he knew the young woman was right, Sir Almas wasn't so certain he could do it. He could not really explain to anyone how he felt; it was like the accident had robbed him of his fighting spirit.

He just did not have the ambition to pursue the things he loved.

He felt like his position as a knight of Oak Land was already lost to him.

Chapter

31

ELLA NEVER GOT HER ANSWER THAT DAY, NOR THE following two weeks that they continued to go for daily walks. Captain Toby informed Sir Almas that he could keep his job as a garrison commander available to him for one more month. Several other candidates were in the testing and review process to replace Sir Almas on the assumption that he would not be returning to his job.

Still, this warning did nothing to motivate the knight.

He has truly given up. Della thought decidedly one day.

Sir Almas would sit out on his chair out in front of the house for hours, doing nothing. He tried to better his situation once, and when he was faced with opposition, he gave up.

What could cause someone so strong-willed as Sir Almas to give up so easily? Della pondered in puzzlement.

Amelia kept out of the house as often as she could, because

she could not bear to watch her strong big brother giving up so easily.

Sir Almas had isolated himself from those who cared the most about him. It was as though every effort to help Sir Almas was for nothing; he rejected and blocked all their attempts.

Della was in the main room folding the linens from the wash earlier that morning. Sir Almas was staying in bed that day because he was not feeling too well. Della did not mind doing household duties, even though she had to do Amelia's share because the other woman was not around to do her part.

In the middle of folding the wash towels, there came a heavy pounding knock on the front door. The sound startled Della so badly that she jumped in surprise and dropped the towel she had been in the middle of folding.

There was still part of her that wanted to run and hide whenever she got frightened.

For a long while she debated on what to do next. She knew that no one else was around to handle the visitor for her.

She thought about arousing Sir Almas, but felt that the knight might not be too pleased if it was for nothing. While she stood there trying to decide on what to do, a second loud knock came.

Summoning all her courage, Della slowly made her way across the room and over to the door.

Again, there came another loud blow.

Taking a deep breath, Della unbolted the door and opened it. She was struck with deep fear at who she saw standing on the opposite side of the threshold.

Sir Missiani stood before her, lavishly dressed and he had a wide sinister grin on his face as he stared at her with vicious greedy eyes.

"Well, well, if it isn't Sir Almas's servant girl." he remarked chuckling as he looked her over with hungry eyes.

"I…I will get Sir Almas." Della stammered her voice quivering as she began to back away.

"No, there's no need to," the knight said forcing the door open with one hand and reached out grasping Della by the arm with his other.

Della let out a small gasp of surprise and tried to twist her arm away. The knight's grip was too strong on her and he pulled her towards him. Della groaned with dread and disgust; pushing against the man's chest when he pulled her to him and hugged her close.

"No! No!" Della cried out knowing what the knight was planning.

"Let me go!" she yelled fighting the tears of desperation.

"No—please!"

She could feel the knight's breath against her face as Sir Missiani began to kiss her neck.

"Get off of me!" she groaned struggling to repel the attacks.

"Come here darling." he bid as he kissed her on the lips.

Bringing her knee up; Della hit the knight in the groin causing him to groan in surprise and double-over in pain.

"Ah—ow." Sir Missiani yelped.

In a moment of anger, he grasped Della by the hair and flung her away from him with all the force he could muster.

Della fell backward uncontrollably, hitting her backside on the floor first. When her head came down, it struck the edge of the wooden couch.

"What do you think happened?" Captain Toby inquired kneeling down beside the couch where there were droplets of dried blood.

"I don't know," Sir Almas muttered worriedly as he paced back and forth.

"I heard some commotion and voices out here. But when I got down here there was no one."

"The door was left open and this was all you found I assume?" the Captain asked motioning to the blood on the floor and discarded towel.

"Yes, yes!" the knight exclaimed in frustration.

"Easy, calm down," his friend beckoned straightening up, he turned to Sir Almas.

"It will do you no good getting upset and angry about what has happened."

"I should have stayed with her—or she should have come over and got me." Sir Almas grumbled rubbing his hands over his face.

"Why didn't she cry out?"

"Maybe she couldn't," Captain Toby suggested.

"Who would come after her, assuming the blood is hers."

"Of course, it is," Sir Almas snapped impatiently.

"If it wasn't, then she would still be here with us and not missing."

"Okay," Captain Toby said in a calming tone. "Begs the question, who in their right mind would want to take her? In broad daylight non the less."

"Who knows!" Sir Almas exclaimed shrugging wearily.

Wherever she is, she will be so frightened. Sir Almas reflected in agony.

This is not right! Who could be so cruel and would want to kidnap her!

"Almas, can you think of anyone who would want to punish you by getting revenge on you?" Captain Toby questioned thinking hard.

"No—you know me, Toby. You know my friends and enemies as well as I do." Sir Almas reasoned.

"There's no—"

The knight trailed off as a horrifying realization struck him.

"What? What's wrong?" the Captain asked noticing the change in his friend's face.

"No, no..." Sir Almas gasped, his face going white as a sheet.

"Almas, what is it?" the Captain pressed anxiously.

"Sir Brutus Missiani." the knight stated flatly.

"What about Brutus. What does he have to do with anything?" Captain Toby asked puzzled.

"I owe him a debt of coin." Sir Almas explained feeling ashamed.

"He came to collect it during the tournament, and I convinced him that I would pay it back after the games...I was counting on my winnings to pay him."

"And you think he came to collect?" Captain Toby asked, not sure he wanted to believe that another knight could do such a heinous act as kidnapping.

"Yes,"

"B—but why take Della?" Captain Toby muttered perplexed.

"Because she was with me when I ran into Brutus at the tournament and he took interest in Della. He offered to take her in exchange for the coin I owe him." Sir Almas sighed running his hands over his face.

"Do you think he would really be that vicious and bold as to take her by force?" Captain Toby asked astonished.

"Absolutely," Sir Almas confirmed without a doubt. "We both no he is a honorless sinister man, who takes what he wants.

I know for a fact, that he has Della."

Chapter

32

ELLA WOKE UP IN A DIMLY LIT ROOM LYING ON HER side, on an icy cold stone floor. The room was empty, with only a small barred window and door. When she tried to use her hands to push off the floor to get into a sitting position, she discovered that they were weighed down by shackles on her wrists.

What is going on?

Della began to feel panic rising up deep down. She had been in chains before, but that was in Varamor and she had been a slave then.

It must be a dream; this cannot be real!

Forcing herself to calm down and concentrate; Della slowly sat up and gazed around the room.

It was shadowy and empty.

Her head ached badly, and any movement sent her head spinning. She reached up and touched the back of her head and found that her hair was damp and sticky. Pulling her hand away from the spot on her head that hurt; Della saw something dark on her fingers and knew that it must be blood.

Suddenly, the events from before came flooding back.

That horrible, wretched knight had viciously attacked her. He had his hands all over her and when she fought back, he pushed her away. Della guessed that when she fell, she must have struck something hard enough to get knocked out.

He must have taken me back to his place and have me locked up in his room.

That means, Sir Almas has no idea where I am or who took me.

She recalled that Sir Almas had owed Sir Missiani a great debt of coin that he came to collect at the tournament. Sir Almas had been able to convince Sir Missiani that he would pay him back after the games, but when Sir Almas had been injured, the debt went unpaid.

By taking me, Sir Missiani must figure it is a fair exchange. A debt paid. Della thought as the horror of the situation she found herself in settled on her.

Sir Missiani had expressed his desire for wanting Della instead of the coin he was owed, but Sir Almas would have none of it. Sir Missiani must have grown inpatient and came to demand his payment from the knight, but encountered Della instead.

He took what he felt was his.

I can't stay here! Della told herself fearfully. *I have to escape—I have to get out **now!***

She slipped into a full panic knowing what plans the devious cruel knight had in mind for her. Della had already suffered through the inhumanity of that way of life and just being trapped in the dark room was enough.

She was in pure agony.

Della rose to her feet and made a desperate mad dash for the door of room. She got two strides before the chains on her wrist were pulled taunt and she was jolted back. The sudden force jerked her back and she fell to her knees with a resounding thud.

"AH!" she screamed in pain.

Tears prickled in her eyes from the stinging pain, but she fought against breaking down completely. She had survived the horrors of slavery once before and she would do it again. Back then, she had no hope of any rescue, no one cared for her.

But now—now she had Sir Almas.

She believed that he would not stop searching for her. Della knew that she would have to be strong enough to hold on, until the knight came for her.

If he can figure out where I am—and who took me. The thought dawned on Della.

Oh, God, Sir Almas knows You and wholly trusts in Your will. Please, please show him the way—if You are really all that he says and believes You are. If what he says about You is true, then I know You will help him.

Please…do this and I shall truly believe in You, just as Sir Almas does.

Della reverently prayed for the first time in her life. She had never believed in a God or the gods of her people—especially not after what she had been put through. She had always been convinced that she was alone in life and if there really was a higher power; then her circumstances should not have been so horrible.

What kind of a God could let that happen?

Though, Della was not so convinced now that God wasn't real, not after she had been around Sir Almas for so long and saw the loving devotion he had for his God. She gradually began to believe that there was a higher power, and maybe—just maybe He cared…even for her.

Why had she been so fortunate to have ended up with such a patient caring man as Sir Almas? How was it possible that she was still alive after everything she had been put through?

If You are real, God, then show me. Della challenged earnestly.

Prayer was all she had left now.

She did not know how long she had been sitting alone in the dark room. There was noise outside of the door as the lock was undone and it was drawn open. A shaft of pale-yellow light pooled into the room, a female figure appeared in the doorway and carried a tray in her hands.

Della sat up and scooted away from the shadowy figure, until her back was pressed against the wall behind her. She pulled her legs up against her chest and hugged her arms around her legs, turning her face away from the woman.

"Hello," the stranger greeted in a light shaken tone.

"Are you hungry?"

Della didn't dare move.

"It's okay," the woman assured her kneeling down next to her and touched Della's arm.

Della flinched away.

"Easy, easy now." the woman beckoned taking a step back.

I won't hurt you—I promise."

Della slowly turned her face toward the woman. The stranger was short in stature, thin and middle-aged, with greying wiry hair. Her face was lined with age and stress, there was a nasty burn scar the had mangled her face.

Beyond all her outward hinderances, there was a genuine sweet kindness in her eyes and Della felt that she could be comfortable around the woman.

"You must be starving." the woman remarked with gentle care, pulling a cloth off the side of the tray.

There was a bowl of stew and bread on the tray, along with a small cup of some kind of dark brown liquid.

"Here, I brought you something."

"W—why am I here?" Della stammered.

"That's not important." the woman reasoned dismissively, avoiding the question.

"Come now, you must eat something."

"Tell me, why I am here!" Della demanded firmly.

The woman only sighed deeply; her hands resting on either side of the tray.

"You are here to be whatever Sir Missiani wishes you to become..." the woman paused wearily.

Della shuttered and closed her eyes tightly; she knew exactly what Sir Missiani wanted her to be.

"For his pleasure," Della finished flatly, her voice barely above a whisper.

"I am so, so sorry." the woman's voice trembled.

Della felt numb all over, her worst nightmare was coming true. She thought she had left her old life behind her, the time in the military camps and years as a slave. She never realized how terribly wrong she was.

"Do as he wants, and you will be treated well." the woman warned through her tears of mourning.

No! Della yelled inwardly, feeling defiant. *I did not comply before and I will not—*

Her train of thought was abruptly interrupted by the sound of a distant door being shoved open and the scuffing sound of boots on stone. The woman beside her whimpered and coward away with her head down.

Della went ridged and braced against the wall; her eyes locked on the figure in the doorway.

It was Sir Missiani.

The knight staggered into the doorway and stood there for a moment, using a hand on the doorframe to steady himself. He was drunk.

With a sinister grin and wicked lustful look in his eyes, the knight stumbled down the steps and moved toward her.

"AHH! NO!" Della screamed hysterically and began to thrash her arms and legs wildly as the knight attacked her.

33

"I MUST ASK, ALMAS, HOW MUCH COIN DO YOU OWE BRUTUS?" Captain Toby requested earnestly.

"A hundred." Sir Almas muttered under his breath.

"A hundred, a hundred what? Coppers, silver—"

"Gold." the knight blurted.

"*A hundred gold?*" the Captain gasped in shock.

Sir Almas nodded numbly, with a sour look on his face.

"Almas, what on earth did you need to borrow that much gold coin for?"

"It was for a worthy cause; I can assure you that." Sir Almas said dodging around the question.

"What kind of a worthy cause?" the Captain pressed.

"It's of little consequence now." Sir Almas said dismissively.

"Almas," Captain Toby's tone was firm. "Tell me, what did you need that much coin for."

"I bought a suit of armor." the knight finally relented.

"A suit of armor?! Almas, why would anyone pay that much for a suit of armor!" Captain Toby exclaimed in stunned shock.

"You got cheated, Almas. Plain and simple."

"No, I didn't." the knight was quick to refute.

"Yes, yes you did."

"No, I did not." the knight punctuated his sentence.

"Yes, you did."

The knight looked away and shook his head in determination.

"Toby, you don't understand," he looked up earnestly. "This was no ordinary suit of armor."

"Come on, Almas, you can get a cheap suit of armor anywhere and it will be just as good as an expensive suit."

"Come with me," Sir Almas invited as he motioned to his bedroom. "I have to show you something."

Captain Toby shrugged as he stood up and followed his friend through the main room and into the bedroom.

"This is why I had to borrow from Brutus, but I swear it was worth it." Sir Almas said pulling his door away from the wall revealing a suit of armor on a stand.

"Oh, wow!" the Captain uttered stunned at what he saw. "Is...it—"

"Yes, it is," Sir Almas confirmed with a nod. "When I saw it at a merchant's booth, I too didn't believe it was real, until I took a closer look."

"A suit of armor from the Knights of Valor," the Captain announced shaking his head in disbelief.

"But, not just any member of the Knights of Valor," Sir Almas noted as he went forward and turn the shoulder strap over to reveal etched in initials.

S. M.

"No way," the Captain stepped forward to get a better look. "It can't be. That's impossible."

"After I purchased it, I brought it to Master Bemithas in Ravens Burg and he was able to confirm that it is indeed the real thing."

"This is the armor that was regularly wore by Sir Marston, personal bodyguard and friend of King Collin and Queen Annabella of Teary Isles." Captain Toby noted astonished.

"You said a merchant here in Oak Land had it?"

"Yes, during the fall festival a few years ago," Sir Almas explained. "He had it on display, that's the only reason it caught my attention. The merchant wasn't smart enough to know what he really had, but he knew enough to realize that it was plated with silver, as was the sword."

"A sword? Don't tell me, you were also able to get a silver sword." Captain Toby could not believe what he was hearing,

"I did," the knight replied pointing to the sword stuck in the scabbard lying underneath the stand. "He knew they both had silver on them and that's why he demanded a hundred gold coins for the set. I hardly had five pieces of gold, as a knight, you know we only make ten gold every six months as our commission. So, I went to Sir Brutus and asked to borrow coin."

"I assume that was back when the two of you were still good friends," the Captain acknowledged. "Does he know about this?"

"Absolutely not! I am not that foolish; besides I know one can be severely punished for owning a Silver Sword without going through the proper channels of getting it passed down to them. Besides, no one should have the armor of Sir Marston in their possession, I keep wondering why he wasn't buried in it."

"Perhaps he was, but his grave was probably looted." the Captain suggested thoughtfully.

"Who would loot the grave of a great hero? A founder of our country." Sir Almas pondered deeply.

"Anyone looking for a quick way to make some coin," the Captain noted.

"It's a wonder that more of the graves of the founders haven't been looted, with stories of jewelry, coins, and valuables being buried with them."

"People used to have decency and respect." the knight muttered under his breath.

"The world has changed." Captain Toby mentioned.

The knight shook his head in disgust.

"So, getting back to the original point," Captain Toby said after a moment of silence.

"You borrowed the gold from Sir Brutus, but hadn't paid any of it back in the time since? Why not, what stopped you?"

"I was gone," Sir Almas replied. "I borrowed the coin some months before the campaign against Varamor took place. I was unable to pay him back, and as you know; he and I had a falling out a few weeks before I departed."

"I see," the Captain acknowledged nodding slowly. "Why didn't you come to me, when you needed coin?"

"I knew you didn't have the amount I required; besides, you would have questioned me until I told you what I needed it for."

"Would it have been so bad if I knew about this?"

"No, not really. Well, you know, you don't have a good mask face. You would have insisted on tagging along when I purchased this, and your enthusiasm would have given away that the armor was worth so much more than a few gold coins."

The Captain did know whether to feel offended or slightly amused with his friend's stark honesty.

"You have a bit of a point there." the Captain reluctantly agreed as he sat down on the edge of the couch.

"So, what's your plan?"

"Plan? Do I need a plan?" Sir Almas demanded enraged. "I know that filthy animal took her! I am going to get her back."

"Almas hold on a minute," Captain Toby interceded sternly.

"You can't just storm into Brutus's home and demand Della. "How can you be certain he has her?"

"Who else would barge into my house and forcibly take Della?"

"I—"

"Huh?! You tell me, if not Brutus, then who!" Sir Almas put to his friend.

"I just want you to carefully consider what you are about to do."

Captain Toby warned cautiously. "Brutus is a very powerful man, with connections to the royal family."

"I care not!" Sir Almas spat furiously.

"I am only trying to tell you to be cautious, Almas. Is this girl really worth risking your career and family name for?"

Sir Almas abruptly stopped pacing the floor and spun on his heels, turning towards his friend.

"How dare you suggest such a thing!" he snapped in a low tone.

"She's not your problem, Almas." the Captain appealed rising to his feet.

"I warned you before that she would only end up causing you trouble and grief."

"A problem?!" Sir Almas took a threatening step toward the Captain.

"You only see her as a problem because she's not a native and she was a slave. What if it had been Amelia and not Della? What would your reaction have been then?"

"You already know the answer to that one." the Captain replied standing toe-to-toe with the knight.

"But Della is different. She doesn't belong here. So, just let everything be as it is. The debt you owed Brutus is settled, the trouble between you two is done."

"Different? *Different?!*" the knight roared furiously.

"Get out of my house—*now* !" the knight growled.

"Almas, please." Captain Toby tried to reason.

"Get out of my sight, I don't want to see you!" Sir Almas yelled in a fit of rage.

"Come on, Almas, listen to reason." the Captain pleaded as he began to back away from the knight.

"Della does not need to be any of your concern anymore. Maybe this is for the best."

"Out!!!" Sir Almas yelled pointing at the door. "I never want to see you again."

"Almas—"

"No, we're done!" Sir Almas abruptly cut him off by throwing his hands up.

"Our friendship is over."

Captain Toby gave Sir Almas a look of sheer crushed devastation; he hesitated in his next move, as if hoping he had not heard right. The knight stood firmly, giving the Captain an icy cold glare.

"You will regret any move against Sir Brutus. Mark my words." Captain Toby muttered before he turned and strode out the door. "Going for that woman is a mistake."

Sir Almas no longer cared what it would cost to get Della back, he had already lost so much. First, his career as a knight, then poor Della, and now his childhood friendship to Captain Toby.

He was far beyond the stage of regret.

I may not be able to control much in my life right now, but I can try to get back one thing I lost. I will find Della—no matter the cost. Sir Almas told himself with conviction.

It's time to make Brutus Missiani pay for what he's done to me... and my family.

Grabbing his sword off the hook beside the front door. Buckling it on, he hurried out the door, not bothering to close it behind him.

Della needed him, and time was of the utmost importance.

Quickly, Sir Almas saddled his warhorse and mounted up. Setting his spurs to his mount, he galloped down the lane, away from his house and toward the wealthy district of the kingdom, where Sir Brutus lived.

He knew he was about to risk everything for a woman he hardly knew. Through the time that they had been together he had begun to get to know her. He began to understand why she was the way she was.

Della's trust was a fragile thing and to make any headway with her, you had to have the patience of Job. Sir Almas knew that there had been a tremendous breakthrough with Della, when he had confessed how much he cared for her.

He had been denying what he was feeling for her since day one.

Only after a few days of having Della in his care, did Sir Almas realize why he felt so drawn to her.

Upon laying eyes on her, he had fallen madly in love with her. Everything about her was beautiful and fascinating. She had brought him such peace and joy that he had not known since before his parents had died.

Even more, she helped him find his personal independence. For too long, he had been doing what was best for everyone around him never once putting himself first. He wondered how much he had missed out on because of this.

His every thought was filled with the woman and he truly felt that he could not live without her. With how traumatized the poor woman had been, no one would have expected her to recover. Somehow, Sir Almas and Della brought out the best in each other.

Della had gone from a scared timid woman to a bubbly curious soul. She caused him to carefully consider every choice he made; he never wanted to upset or disappoint her. To see her in tears over anything was almost too heart-wrenching to take.

We still have a long way to go in our relationship; so much to learn from and about each other, Sir Almas reflected getting choked up as he rode along.

She trusts me wholly and I will not leave or abandon her.

I do not care what people think about us. Della is every bit my responsibility because she's the woman I love.

I will not allow Brutus to take her from me and have his way with her. She's a human being—not an object!

Villagers traveling along the alleyways and streets had to quickly move out of the way as Sir Almas came riding through. He received glares and dirty looks; some people yelled complaints at him as he galloped past. The knight only ignored them and kept going.

Della had been absent for a day and that had already been too long.

There had been a small spot of blood on the floor of the house near the couch. If Della had been hurt, how bad was it? Was it life-threatening or just a small scratch?

What if Della had been killed?

No, no! Sir Almas pushed the horrible possibility away.

I doubt that Brutus would go through the trouble of killing her. No, he wants to punish me, so he will let her live for a while.

The way he looked upon her at the tournament, told the knight that the man had sinister sick plans for the young woman. A suffocating panic began to swell up in his throat at the very thought of what Sir Brutus's intentions for Della were.

Finally, he rode over the narrow bridge of the entrance of Sir Brutus's mansion. Slowing his mount to a canter as he came into the front yard; two of Sir Brutus's guards were alerted and approached the knight.

Hardly, had his mount slowed to a trot when Sir Almas swung down from the saddle. As soon as his feet touched the cobblestones; Sir Almas released the reins and drew his sword. The guards went on the defensive, giving Sir Almas hard looks, they reached for their weapons ready to engage.

"My business does not concern you," Sir Almas warned as he strode in their direction. "I have come for what is mine. Don't stand in my way unless you plan on dying."

Both held their ground, hands on their weapons ready to draw. Seeing the hard look in the knight's eyes and judging by his mannerisms; they knew he was serious and determined.

"Stand down." the older guard told the other as he removed his hand from his weapon and motioned for the other man to do the same.

The other man was tense and reluctant at first, but eventually lowered his shoulders and relented.

Sir Almas didn't worry about the men as he marched between them and toward the front door of the split-level mansion.

He was getting his Della back!

Chapter

34

THE SERVANTS OF THE HOUSE UPON SEEING SIR ALMAS with his sword drawn; fled from him in fright. Striding along, Sir Almas seized the tunic collar of the cowering house butler.

"P—please, Sir, don't hurt me." the man begged holding his hand up.

"The woman—Della, where is she?!" Sir Almas demanded giving the servant a hard look.

"W—woman? I have no knowledge of a woman named Della." the man replied.

"Your master, he brought a woman here. I know he did." Sir Almas countered. "Now, tell me where she is."

"I don't know!" the man shouted his voice quivering with petrified fear.

Sir Almas was infuriated and felt that the servant must be lying to him.

"Are you searching for a young girl?" a soft voice called out from across the room.

Sir Almas's eyes tore away from the man held in his grip. At the top of the stairs of the second floor, was a middle aged, half-starved woman in a filthy dress looking down at him with a stony gaze.

"Y—yes, do you know where she is?" Sir Almas asked eagerly.

"Yes," the woman replied. "I can take you to her."

Sir Almas released the house butler and headed up the stairs towards the woman. The woman didn't seem to be very fearful of the knight; rather she seemed eager to help him. she led him up another narrow stairway and down a corridor and through a bedroom and sitting room.

They entered a drafty part of the mansion. This area was ill furnished and most of the windows were boarded up and it looked as though the rooms hadn't been used in a long time.

Down at the end of the long-cobwebbed narrow, dark hallway was a door. The door was short and wide, but thickly layered with grime. The woman stopped at the door and turned to Sir Almas.

"It's locked." she informed him.

"Where's the key?" the knight asked impatiently.

"Sir Missiani has them." the woman replied lowering her head.

"Argh!" Sir Almas snapped slamming a fist against the door frame in frustrated anger.

"Where is he?"

"Attending his duties as a council member." she answered.

"When do you expect him back?"

"Anytime."

"Good," Sir Almas said with a hint of pleasure.

How I would love to thrash him senseless.

"Back up." he warned her as he stepped up to the door.

Looking down at the sword clenched in Sir Almas' hand and she immediately knew what he was going to do. She stepped behind the knight, clearing the swing of his sword, she turned her face away to prevent her face being struck by any flying debris.

Lifting the sword; Sir Almas swung as hard as he could at the door, with the first few strikes the sword only seemed to bounce off the door. Taking a harder swing with all the force he could muster; Sir Almas cracked his sword against the door.

A chunk of wood came out of the door. Seeing that he had made a little headway; Sir Almas swung more forcefully and vigorously. He was desperate to get into the room, to see Della. Chopping into the door was made difficult by this bum arm, his swings were not as forceful or effective as they otherwise could have been.

I have to get to the woman I care about!

It took several minutes of hard hits to get through the door, but eventually he was able to make a hole large enough to climb through.

The room was shadowy and smelled horribly of mold and sweat. Handing his sword to the woman standing behind him, Sir Almas made his way through the crude opening. He felt that he could trust the woman to hang onto his sword, without having to worry about her trying to cause him any harm.

As soon as he entered the room, he could hear the hysterical screams of a young woman, the tone of her voice left no doubt in his mind that it was Della. He could make out her shadowy form curled up in the far corner of the room.

She half-backed up the wall, thrashing her arms and legs in mad panic. She was deathly afraid of Sir Almas. The knight didn't have to try hard to figure out what Sir Missiani had put poor Della through already.

The knight's stomach turned at the realization of what Sir Missiani had taken Della for, his heart broke at the sight of her.

"No, no! Get away from me!" Della cried out.

"Della, Della. It's me," the knight reasoned gently as he tried to calm her down.

"It's Sir Almas."

He got down on his knees as soon as he got close to her, she never stopped kicking or screaming. As he slowly reached towards her, she began to scratch and slap at his hands. His heart ached and he was horrified to find that she had no clothes.

Seeing her in this way, made him feel like he was lesser of a knight and man. He felt that he failed her, failed to protect her.

That monster! Sir Almas spat inwardly; his anger burned toward Sir Missiani.

"NO!" Della wailed hysterically.

Pausing, Sir Almas reached up and unclasped his cloak and pulled it off. Holding it between his hands; he came toward Della once more.

Still she scratched and kicked at him.

Quickly, he closed the distance between them and wrapped the cloak around her like a blanket, restraining her arms. Della trembled violently and sobbed wretchedly as the knight pulled her into his protective embrace. Hugging his head close to hers, he leaned in close to whisper into her ear.

"Easy, easy now. Shush." he said softly. "It's all right. You are safe now. I'm here."

Della wriggled about a few more times, but gradually her fighting began to subside when she discovered she could not hardly move. She went limp in his arms before cuddling her face against his chest and sobbed uncontrollably; at last, recognizing who held her.

"You're safe now."

I am going to kill him! the knight promised himself as he allowed his tears to fall onto her dirtied black hair.

Chapter

35

Sir Almas let Della take her time to calm down and relax with him before he convinced her that they had to move. Even when the knight went to stand up, Della clung to him and her head was pressed tightly against his chest, hiding her face.

Wrapping his cloak around the young woman so that it properly covered her, he carefully gathered her up in his arms. The servant woman ducked out of the room ahead of them. Sir Almas had to carefully navigate his way out of the opening in the door; he was forced to duck so low that he was nearly crawling on his knees.

Della had an arm wrapped around his neck and her other under his arm, holding on tightly to him so that he did not have to worry about hanging onto her for the moment.

Della was not letting go.

The poor young woman was dirty, bloodied and severely bruised.

Her long raven-black hair was matted, filthy, and badly tangled. She was in a worse state then when Sir Almas rescued her from the camp of the army of Millet—and it all happened in less than two days!

Fortunately, Sir Almas didn't encounter Sir Missiani as he exited the mansion. Sir Almas knew that if he had run into Sir Missiani at that moment, nothing in the world would restrain his hand. He was filled with such burning anger that he would have no remorse in striking the other knight down.

When he got outside, he quickly realized that it would be next to impossible to try and mount his horse while holding onto Della. He knew that she would not let him go long enough for him to mount his horse; she was too frightened and hurting to do so.

I will just have to carry her home. he resolved grimly.

"Woman," he addressed the woman who had helped him.

"Yes, sir." The woman said standing at attention before him, still holding his sword.

"Can you bring my horse and follow me home?" he asked. "I will give you coin worth your time."

"N—no, Sir. I must not." the woman replied her voice quivering.

"Worry not about Sir Brutus, he will not lay a finger on you." the knight assured her firmly. "You can leave his service and stay with me...if you wish."

"He will come for me," she insisted. "Told me I could never leave his service, he did."

"No, I will make certain that he never comes for you. You have my word as a knight." Sir Almas promised her.

The woman stood where she was; by the expression on her face, Sir Almas could tell that she was carefully considering his offer.

"Please, I don't want to leave you here," the knight pleaded.

"You have helped me and for it, I fear that Sir Missiani will either severely punish or kill you for it."

"Please...come   with   us."
"Very well, I shall come," the woman reluctantly gave in.

"But I only come because of the girl. The way you care for her is passionate—and rare."

Sir Almas nodded his head in gracious thanks.

"Here, you can slip that back into the scabbard." the knight said turning his left side toward her.

The woman stepped up and carefully put the sword back in its rightful place.

"Thank you."

Sir Almas waited until the woman led his mount up close to him, before he set off down the road in the direction of the poorer district of the city, where home was. When he arrived at home with Della and the woman in tow; Amelia was waiting for him on the front porch. Captain Toby stood behind her; holding her shoulders as she sobbed with worry for her brother.

Seeing her brother approaching with the two women; she rose from her chair and rushed out to meet them.

"Oh, my!" she gasped in shock. "What has happened?"

Fearfully, Della's grip tightened around the knight, and she let out a low terrified whimper.

"Whoa, Amelia, stop now!" Sir Almas called out to her waving her off with his free hand.

"What? What is it, what's the matter?" Amelia stammered stopping short, giving her brother a puzzled look.

"Don't get too close." he explained with a tone of pleading.

"Why?" Amelia sounded hurt.

"She's been put through so much," the knight began, but struggled with how to explain what happened to Della. "So, much pain and agony. Too many people may be overwhelming for her right now."

For the first time, Amelia's eyes drifted down to the woman that was bundled in her brother's arms. Her expression went from a frown of deep concern to white with shock.

"Oh, Almas!" she gasped with pity bringing a hand to cover her mouth.

"You mean she's been—"

Sir Almas vigorously nodded, though the very thought deeply pained him.

"Oh!" Amelia muttered tears coming to her eyes. "Who d—did this?"

"Who do you think?" Sir Almas shot back angrily. "That filthy creature, **Brutus**!"

"No…it can't be." Amelia stammered in disbelief. "Surely, he couldn't be so vicious and ill mannered."

"Yes, he could be—and he did." The knight shot back icily. "He took her as payment for the debt I owed him. I always knew he was a man of lowly character, but never imagined he could be so—sick!"

"How could he do such awful things?" Amelia pondered in astonishment.

"How is it that everyone in this kingdom treats Della and her people as lesser humans? To Sir Missiani, Della is only an object to be brutalized and used up before being discarded like a piece of waste!" Sir Almas pointed out, all the frustration and anger he was holding back rushed forth.

"No one cares about Della's safety or needs—all they can see is a slave! It's like no one can move beyond *that!*"

"That's not true Almas." His sister attempted to reason.

"Not true? Ha! You and Toby warned me against taking Della on, you kept saying how much trouble and heartache she would bring me. Relentlessly, you both tried to get me to send her away, because she means nothing to you!

And you," Sir Almas' tone became low and icy as he glared at the Captain.

"You suggested the worst thing of all! To leave her in the hands of that—that animal!!!"

Looking over her shoulder, Amelia shot her fiancée a look of shock, and the Captain could only look away in shame and shrugged.

"We only cared about your wellbeing and future, Almas, we know having the girl here with us would only cause trouble." Amelia continued to reason.

"And it has," Captain Toby interceded.

"How is this—any of this, her fault?" Sir Almas demanded

nodding his head in the direction of the woman in his arms. "Why is everything bad that happens to us is somehow her fault or mine?"

"Almas, it is her very presence here that is a problem. She is a Varamorean. Her people are not welcome here." Captain Toby said pointedly.

"Not welcome here?" Sir Almas chuckled sarcastically; he could not believe what he was hearing.

"Why? What has she…an innocent young woman ever done to us?"

"Nothing," Captain Toby answered lowering his head in shame. "It's not customary to have one of them here with us."

"Why are you even speaking to me?" Sir Almas demanded bitterly, narrowing his eyes at the Captain. "I thought I told you I never wanted to see you again."

"Almas, he's my fiancée and soon-to-be your brother," Amelia scolded in astonishment.

"So? He treated her with disrespect," the knight shot back. "Something I will not tolerate."

"Almas, Toby is only concerned for you. Keeping the woman around is against traditional rules."

"You two make me sick," Sir Almas said with strong distaste. "It's not the people of Oak Land that I have to protect from Della— it's Della that I have to protect from people like you two."

Captain Toby and Amelia stared at Sir Almas in shock and offense.

"I don't want Della to have to live all her life being seen as an object and not human. To have to fear being taken advantage of for the rest of her life.

She doesn't need that because she has value," he insisted passionately.

"She's a human being—a young woman. And…and I love her."

Amelia suddenly gasped in surprise at this revelation, a look of scandal came over her face and she frowned at her brother in disappointment.

"You—you can't possibly mean that." Amelia stammered in stubborn denial.

"I am very serious," Sir Almas confirmed, unwaveringly he added.

"I love this woman. I love her for everything about her, but mostly because she's honest-more than either of you have been."

"Almas!" his sister began to scold.

"No! You can both leave us. You sister, can go and pack your things and get out of my house!" Sir Almas ordered sternly.

"You can come back when you learn to look beyond your prejudices and self-interests. I will welcome you back when you find it within yourself to support us and are ready to look at this woman as an equal!" Sir Almas indicated nodding to the trembling woman he cradled in his arms.

"You will regret this!" his sister spat with an icy glare.

Captain Toby took her hand in his and they both gave Sir Almas and Della looks of disappointment as they stormed past.

Chapter

36

ITH THE GENTLE CARE THAT SOMEONE WOULD show an infant; Sir Almas carried Della into the house and sat her down on the edge of his bed.

"Della? Della, are you listening to me?' Sir Almas asked craning his head down to look into her face.

Slowly, she lifted her bruised, mud smeared face and looked into his eyes. Her face reflected that of fear, her eyes were wide and uncertain.

"I need to leave you in the care of this woman," he explained glancing up at the woman who stood in the doorway.

"She'll help you clean up and dress, okay?"

Della didn't say a word, but started to shake. The woman came forward and quickly took up a position beside the knight. Sir Almas carefully peeled her arms off from around his neck and under his arm.

"What is your name?" he asked the woman.

"Marie, Marie Valto." the woman answered obediently.

"Good," the knight acknowledged trying to pull away from Della's grasp gradually.

"Go slowly; she's terrified of everyone."

"No! No!" she began to scream desperately as she reached out and snatched the edge of his cloak.

"Della, it's okay." Sir Almas tried to assure her. "Don't worry, I'm not going anywhere, I will be waiting right outside for you."

"No, don't leave!" she sobbed her eyes flashed with deep fear. "Please..."

"I can't be in here while you—you get changed." the knight reasoned awkwardly.

He already felt like he had invaded her privacy when he broke her out of the cell and saw her nakedness. He felt it was so wrong for him to have seen her in that state, especially when they were not wed.

The young woman looked up at him with her big frightened fawn eyes, holding tightly to his sleeve.

"Please!" she pleaded tears ran down her face, her anxious eyes settled on the knight.

"I—"

"Don't worry about a thing," Marie assured him patiently as she held up her hands. "You stay, just look away when I say to.

Just don't leave, she's not ready for that. Sir Missiani did the unforgiveable to her and broke her spirit. She needs you right now."

The older woman laid a hand of comfort on the knight's arm and gave him a knowing look.

"She trusts you," the woman reaffirmed.

Sir Almas was torn between leaving the woman to her privacy or staying with her. One look at the young woman and Sir Almas knew that his decision was already made for him.

"Very well," Sir Almas relented sitting back down on the edge of the bed.

As soon as he sat down, Della scooted across the bed edge until her thigh was against his and she leaned into his shoulder.

She nuzzled her delicate head against his shoulder, but never stopped trembling all over.

What has Brutus done to you? You seemed so strong and unbreakable before.

Sir Almas pondered mournfully.

You were not in this bad of a state when we rescued you from the camp of the enemy.

Marie left the room for a short while before returning with a basin of cool water and a few washcloths. The knight took one of the cloths and dipped it in the water before he brought it up to Della's face. Knowing his intentions; Della lifted her face towards him and allowed him to wash her face. Whenever the cloth came in contact with a cut or bruise Della would wince in pain.

"I am sorry." Sir Almas apologized with each time she winced.

Working from her forehead down to her nose and lips, the knight gently cleaned her face. As the cloth wiped away the dirt from the corner of her mouth; Della looked up and locked eyes with Sir Almas.

Even though she was trembling something fierce, her eyes were filled with complete trust.

Suddenly, she reached her free hand up and grasped his wrist that held the cloth against her face. Della's gaze never left Sir Almas's eyes; she leaned up towards him and pressed her lips to his.

Kissing the man that she counted as her protector and savior.

The man she loved.

Chapter

37

ELLA NEVER TOOK HER HAND OFF THE KNIGHT'S sleeve, even when Marie helped her dress. When she had to put that hand through a sleeve, she seized his arm with her other hand, not willing to allow him to slip away from her.

She feared that it was all just a dream and that she would wake up any moment and find herself still imprisoned in the room of horrors. She was deathly afraid of letting her knight go. When it came to sleeping that night; Sir Almas couldn't coax her into letting him go. Therefore, he was forced to sleep in the same room and bed as her.

Sir Almas could not sleep, though, he couldn't stop thinking about what Sir Missiani had done to Della. He kept rehearsing in his mind what he planned to do to Brutus once he had his hands on him.

Brutus only deserves one fate, Sir Almas decided. *Death—and even that is too good for a monster like him.*

Sir Almas looked over at the young woman, sleeping fretfully next to him, his sleeve grasped in her thin hand. Her body would tremble every now and again and she would let out a low frightened whimper.

Poor little thing, he thought sorrowfully. *You've been put through so much…how much more must you take?*

When morning came, Sir Almas ate a light breakfast, with Della still clinging to him for dear life. He didn't have to worry about dressing, for he had slept in his uniform and armor throughout the night. He was stiff and sore from sleeping in armor, but looking at the woman at his side he knew that it was all worth it

Della refused to even eat a bite of her breakfast, causing Sir Almas great concern.

Giving Marie a written letter; he sent her off to fetch Priest Lumis. The knight prayed to God that the young woman would be able to be comfortable enough to stay with the Priest while he took care of some personal business.

Lord, please give me the wisdom and strength to know how to deal with Della. To help her understand that I mean her well and that Priest Lumis is a friend that would never harm her.

Please, God, I need Your help! the knight prayed earnestly.

After breakfast, Sir Almas and Della went out to the front porch. He sat down in his wicker chair and lifted the young woman into his lap. She wrapped her arms around him and laid her head against his chest.

One thing Sir Almas noted that morning, was that Della had stopped trembling, even though she let out a soft whimper now and again.

To Sir Almas, it seemed that the kiss he received from Della had signaled a change in their relationship. The last barrier of defense between them had been broken down. Their feelings for each other had been made known and they now trusted each other unconditionally.

As the morning sun came up and warmed them; Della began to

swing a foot back and forth in a relaxed manner. She was completely comfortable and began to hum a sweet faint tune. Sir Almas still felt deep apprehension, but on the surface, he held a warm feeling of pride and love.

Gradually the sun warmed Sir Almas so much that he began to drift off. He was nearly asleep when the sound of boots scraping on the cobblestones caught his attention.

The knight's eyes snapped open, suddenly he defensively reached for his sword that was leaning up against his chair.

"Hey, hey, easy lad!" a calm voice soothed quickly.

Focusing on the figures before them; the knight recognized one as Marie and the other was Priest Lumis, but they weren't alone. There was another man, he looked to be in his mid-twenties, clean shaven and dressed in dull grey priestly robes. There was an air of wisened kindness about him, his dark eyes full of depth and understanding.

Pulling his hand away from his sword handle, Sir Almas relaxed a little, but during his sudden reaction, Della had wrapped her arms tightly around him in fright.

"Priest Lumis," he declared his tone filled with relief. "Thank you for coming."

Priest's Lumis' brow was creased with deep concern as he gazed upon them.

"Almas, this is my good friend and apprentice, Dutton." he motioned to the silent mam beside him. "He hails from the kingdom of Brooklyn Falls."

At this the younger man bowed his head respectfully and Sir Almas only nodded anxiously.

"Almas, what has Sir Missiani done to her?" the Priest gasped in shock as he closely studied the young woman.

Sir Almas struggled to reply; he could not bring himself to explain all that had been done to Della. All he could do was shake his head with a grave expression on his face and looked down.

"Fret not, lad." the Priest assured him in an understanding tone. "No words are needed."

The Priest stepped up to them, he knelt on one knee and reached for the young woman. When his fingers touched her shoulder, the woman instinctively flinched away timidly.

"Easy. It's okay." Priest Lumis soothed gently. "I mean you no harm, child."

Hearing the familiar friendly voice of the Priest, Della turned away from Sir Almas's chest and looked up at the older man.

"Child, you will have to sit with me for a time," Priest Lumis patiently explained. "Sir Almas must go and take care of a few vitally important tasks."

Della hugged against the knight at the very mention of them being separate from one another.

"Della," Sir Almas spoke tipping her chin up with his fingers, so that she looked him in the eyes.

"I have to leave for a short time, I have very important business to settle and I cannot take you with me.

That is why I called upon Priest Lumis—you remember him, don't you?"

Della nodded her head downward.

"He won't hurt you nor will he allow any harm to come to you." Sir Almas continued to explain. "He will just stay here with you and will keep you safe until I return. I promise you with all my heart that I will come back.

You will never be alone again…I promise."

Della took a shuttering breath as she slowly looked from the knight to Priest Lumis and gave a consenting nod.

"Good, very good." Sir Almas approved.

"Come to me, child." Priest Lumis beckoned holding his arms wide.

Della embraced Sir Almas tightly for a few moments before she reluctantly let him go and stood up. She turned to the Priest, and reaching out she took his hand instead of hugging him as she had done with Sir Almas.

"Tal," Sir Almas' tone was edged with anxious apprehension.

"Please, guard her with your life."

"Fear not, Almas." the Priest promised. "She is safe with me—no one will touch her again that has cruel intentions in mind for her. She will be safe with me."

"Good, thank you." the knight sighed with relief as he rose to his feet and took up his sword.

"Almas," Priest Lumis spoke. "Do you want Dutton to accompany you?"

"No," the knight firmly shook his head. "I can handle this alone."

"Almas," the Priest said.

"Yes?" the knight stiffened up slightly and looked to his friend.

"Where are you going?"

"To settle a score."

"With whom?" Priest Lumis asked, though he was certain he already knew the answer.

"With Brutus Missiani." the knight replied with hatred laced words.

"Almas, please don't set out on the road of revenge and do something you will regret. Revenge is not the way."

"Brutus must pay for what he has done to her," the knight lashed out, jabbing a finger at Della.

"I have to kill him."

"You cannot! Think about the girl."

"I am!" Sir Almas shouted. "Brutus kidnapped and brutalized Della. He had her locked in a dark room and beat her—what he did is unforgiveable!

Della deserves justice!"

"At the edge of your sword?"

"Yes!"

"No, you need to go to the authorities."

"The authorities?! Brutus will just pay them off and get away with what he has done."

"I will stand as a witness and you have Marie as well."

"No, Brutus will have no chance of escape. Killing him is the only way to ensure that he pays for his crimes."

"Please!" Della's quivering voice rang out.

Both men stopped their heated arguing and turned their attention to her.

"Almas, please don't kill him."

"But Della, he took advantage of you and did—such horrible things to you and he must pay." Sir Almas insisted.

"Not in your way." the young woman countered.

She reached out and laid a hand of restraint on the hand that he held his sword in.

"You once told me not to be angry or hate those who wronged me because it won't do me any good." Della reasoned. "That forgiveness was ours to give, because Jesus forgives us of all our sins—big or small, if we ask it of Him."

"Didn't you tell me that it was God's responsibility to pass judgment on others and not us? Revenge is wrong and justice is not yours to take by the sword."

Sir Almas was cut deep by Della's truthful words and wisdom.

"Sir Missiani must pay for his crimes, yes," Della insisted as she looked at him with pleading in her eyes. "But in the correct way."

Sir Almas's anger burned with such fury that every fiber of his being was telling him to claim revenge on Sir Missiani himself and not wait around for the council of Oak Land to do it. But, by the pleading in the eyes of the woman he loved and, in his heart, it was telling him to do the right thing.

Justice at the edge of the sword was not right. He would face either time in prison or even be put to death for killing a fellow knight of the realm.

"Listen to her, Almas." the Priest encouraged. "You must not take the law into your own hands.

Sir Missiani has committed at least three crimes. He forcefully took Della, imprisoned her along with others and violated her. Think about it, lad—illegal enslavement is a crime in all Teary Isles. He will have to stand trial before the King himself."

Sir Almas listened intently to Master Lumis' advice and understood that Sir Missiani would face a harsh prison sentence— if not execution. Brutalizing Della and enslavement had a high price on them in terms of punishment for those who committed them.

Either way, life for Sir Brutus Missiani was over as he knew it, and powerful friends couldn't help him out of this one.

"Go to the Marshal with your claim and we will be your witnesses." the Priest urged.

"Very well," Sir Almas relented.

"It may not feel like enough for what he did to Della, but at least things will be done the right way. One day you will come to see that Almas."

Sir Almas nodded numbly; his anger had not subsided.

"I will go and plead my case." he informed them. "I shall return later this evening."

Della anxiously watched as Sir Almas walked down the lane away from his home, away from her. She felt worried for him, hoping, and praying that he would not enact his revenge, but that he would do the right thing.

God, my God. Della prayed in earnest as she looked heavenward.
Go with Sir Almas and restrain his hand. Show him the right way. Please…please, keep him safe.

Chapter

38

"PRISON WAS NOT GOOD ENOUGH FOR THE LIKES OF Brutus Missiani." Sir Almas reflected bitterly.

Several days later, he and Priest Lumis sat around the hearth at the knight's home. It was later in the evening and Della was sound asleep in her own room with Marie. It took a few days, but she finally felt comfortable enough to sleep alone in her own room, but only when Marie was sleeping in a cot next to her bed.

Sir Almas had to stay nearby as well.

"Maybe," Priest Lumis muttered lighting his pipe. "But at least he is locked away, where he can no longer hurt anyone."

"What he did to Della cannot be undone."

"Being angry about it won't do you any good."

"I can't help it," the knight said throwing his hands up. "Della never deserved what happened to her."

"No one does." Priest Lumis inserted.

"But it happened and there is nothing we can do to change that."

"Nothing can change what happened to her then, but I can change our future." the knight said firmly.

"What are you talking about, Almas?" the Priest asked puzzled.

"I am tired of hearing and seeing how people of this kingdom treat Della," Sir Almas began to rant in annoyance.

"They don't see her as an equal human and many only want to take advantage of her, based solely on the fact that she is not a native and they don't believe the same laws apply to her.

I was only kidding myself if I ever thought the people of this kingdom would accept her as one of their own over time. We have been here at home for quite some time and nothing has changed. Honestly, I don't believe it ever will."

"What are you planning on doing about it?" the Priest asked with interest.

"I am not sure yet, but have been seriously considering on leaving here." Sir Almas replied in frustration.

"Leave? And go where?" the Priest was devastated by the news.

"I don't know." Sir Almas said with a shrug.

"Anywhere, as long as Della can live in peace and be happy. Some place where she would not have to be judged for existing or having to worry about being taken advantage of.

Somewhere…where she'll be accepted."

Getting up out of his chair, the knight thoughtfully rubbed his chin and paced the floor.

"Be realistic, Almas," Priest Lumis countered knowingly. "You will only be running from your troubles."

"This is the one time I could live with running from my problems. Besides, getting away from here would be better than the future she faces now." the knight exclaimed.

"She can't go anywhere out in public without someone scaring her or trying to have their way with her!

How long does she have to go through life like this?"

The Priest knew that his friend was right on all accounts about the kind of life the young woman now faced. The kingdom of Oak

Land had stiff, prejudice and unwelcoming people and they could be overly cruel at times—especially to anyone from the land of Varamor. The peoples of Oak Land had suffered greatly at the hands of Varamor's small armies that swept through the area from time to time. The deep resentment was evident whenever they encountered a native of the enemy country.

"You knew full well that Della would face opposition when you brought her here." the Priest reminded.

"Yes, I did. But I never expected anything like this." Sir Almas said turning his attention toward the Priest.

"Do you know that almost everyone I know is against me having that girl under my care? They speak of her like she is the plague or poor fortune."

"I don't feel that way about her." Priest Lumis countered quickly.

"I feel that you have both been good for each other. How would I put it…made for each other as God intended."

Priest Lumis demonstrated his point by interlocking his fingers in each other.

"I know that, Tal." Sir Almas gently scolded as a smile flickered across his face.

"It's just…so annoying how people treat her."

"Did you ever think that perhaps they are judging both of you? That they might be jealous of your happiness?" Priest Lumis challenged raising a brow.

Sir Almas stopped pacing and gave his friend a puzzled look.

"You've been making decisions for yourself ever since you brought her here. You based your choices on what is best for you and her. You are no longer doing whatever people want you to.

You have found your independence because of that young woman and she learned true love and trust from you."

"I have noticed as of late that your sister is most troubled by the young woman's presence," the Priest described.

"I truly believe that she cannot help this, after all, she has been used to having your full undivided attention for all these years."

"I've noticed that as well," Sir Almas agreed. "She and I used to have squabbles off and on—you know the normal sibling kind. But since Della moved in, we have fought nearly every time we speak… and most of it revolves around Della being here."

"Do not trouble yourself about this too much," Priest Lumis advised patiently. "The relationship between you and your sister is changing and these obstacles are growing pains. Over time things will get better…or the two of you will grow apart entirely.

"You see, you are developing into a man that is putting the woman he loves romantically for ahead of what others want or expect. These changes will be difficult to those closest to you."

Sir Almas nodded slowly as it began to dawn on him that he had been putting Della first in almost all his decisions as of late.

Shouldn't she come first?

"What is your heart telling you to do?" the Priest proposed.

"To do whatever I must to ensure Della lives a normal happy life—even if it means we have to move." Sir Almas replied earnestly.

"Then don't stray from what your instincts are telling you," Priest Lumis encouraged.

"Because that woman's happiness is yours as well.

You two are bonded now and only you can break that bond—no one else."

"What do *you* recommend I do?" the knight asked hoping for guidance.

"That is all up to you," Priest Lumis replied holding his hands up before himself.

"All I ask, is that you give things a little time and thought. Moving away will be a big—life-altering decision and should not be taken lightly."

"I won't take this as a light affair." the knight assured with a firm look.

"Good." The Priest approved with a nod as he leaned back in his chair, before adding with a tone of longing sorrow.

"Because, I would hate to see you leave…both of you."

Chapter

39

OBY DID NOT HOLD SIR ALMAS' POSITION IN THE service to the kingdom open for him and the knight found that he was out of a trade. He was a knight without a kingdom to serve. Unexpectantly, Priest Lumis' guest came through for him in two ways. Leaving Della in the living area of the cottage with Marie to prepare evening meal; Sir Almas stepped outside upon request by Dutton.

The young apprentice stood with his back to the front door of the cottage, hands clasped behind him and gazed off into the horizon where the orange sun was sinking low.

"You asked for my attention?" Sir Almas said wanting to get to the matter as soon as possible.

"Hmmm, I did," Dutton nodded patiently.

"As I've come to understand it, you and your friend Captain Falkner had a…falling out?"

"Yes," the knight tensely confirmed not wanting to rehash the past events that ended a long friendship.

"Feelings toward the Captain are bitter, yes?"

"Of course."

"May I ask why?"

"Why what? Why I am still angry with him or why were no longer friends?" Sir Almas snapped peevishly.

"Both." Dutton answered.

"Excuse me, but why is this any of your business?" the knight was quite annoyed by now with the young apprentice's vagueness.

"It's not," Dutton said facing Sir Almas, his expression became serious and brooding.

"I just want to have a better picture of what is going on around here before I lend some advice."

I don't think I need it. Sir Almas thought.

"The answer to both questions is the same," Sir Almas replied working his jaw, thinking about what happened between him and Toby left a bad taste in his mouth.

"When we discovered that Della had been abducted and discussed how to handle the matter, Toby suggested the most debase vile thing I thought I would ever hear come out of anyone's mouth."

Dutton lent his full attention.

"His suggestion was to leave everything as it was, to—to leave Della in Sir Missiani's possession," Sir Almas felt fury burning in his chest and clenched his fists.

"Toby told me that all the young woman has been was troublesome and that it would be somehow for the better if she be left with that—savage. He said that my debt to Sir Missiani was paid in full, as if Della was some object to be owned!"

"Easy," Dutton appealed soothingly. "Don't need to lose your head now, I am not your enemy."

The knight sucked in a deep breath, fighting to keep the swell of frustration and anger down.

"I see," Dutton nodded thoughtfully. "Your reaction and anger are understandable, for the Captain to suggest such a thing is…uncouth.

Do not allow your anger to grow. What was said is in the past and cannot be undone but must be remember that they were only words."

"Only words? Toby meant for us to act upon them!" Sir Almas snapped irritated that Dutton seemed to be dismissing the seriousness of the matter.

"Calm yourself now," Dutton reasoned. "I have not finished."

"What I am trying to convey is that you should not dwell on the way your friend wronged you or this issue will only grow. The wedge between you two will become too great to be moved beyond or reconciled."

Sir Almas paused letting the words sink in. Dutton had a very valid point. Whenever he recalled the incident between him and Toby, he reminded himself of the anger he felt, and his hatred only grew.

Toby had been his best friend since childhood, though, what he said about Della would not be forgotten or easily reconciled, he would hate for it to drive them apart permanently.

Toby was family.

"I know," Sir Almas hung his head resignedly.

"Take time to reflect on what has happened, then pray earnestly about how to manage the matter. Try to repair your friendship and put your mind at ease. Make peace with Toby, if possible."

"I will try," the knight promised. "I don't think it will be right away, the wound is too fresh."

"Understandable," Dutton nodded. "I strongly dislike seeing strained or broke ties. Years of friendship ought to bear so much importance that they are difficult to break and forget."

Sir Almas nodded in agreement and looked down at the stone path. Patching things up with Toby would be difficult and doing it alone would not be possible. He needed the help and guidance of his Almighty Father more than anything.

"Might I suggest one more thing?" Dutton spoke resuming his usually wisened calm.

"Go ahead." Sir Almas shrugged.

"Since you are now without a commission. Try your hand at work as a Sword-for-Hire."

"Excuse me?" Sir Almas looked up at the other man as if he lost his mind.

"A Sword-for-Hire? I was a knight, Dutton; a position that garnered honesty, loyalty and honor. Being a Sword-for-Hire is like trading a baby for a mutt. They bear such an unsavory reputation for good reason, you know."

"I know," Dutton remarked a smile playing at the corners of his mouth.

"But remember, not all Sword-for-Hire's are honorless, self-serving men; just as not all knights are trustworthy and brave."

"You got me there," the knight reluctantly relented. "But why that?"

"A Sword-for-Hire or bodyguard for merchants and tradesmen would suit a man of your abilities the best. That, and you would not have to stray too far from home or be under the authority of a superior. Essentially, you are your own master." Dutton explained.

"True," Sir Almas gave it some thought. "Getting started in the trade will not come easy and this...this ailment won't do me any favors."

Sir Almas motioned to his lame arm.

"Ah, but that is where I come in," Dutton spoke raising a finger.

"I know a few patrons that are interested in the services of a Sword-for-Hire that can promise honesty, loyalty, and adequate protection. With their good word, your future in the trade will be cemented."

Sir Almas gave the apprentice an auspicious gaze; smiling he shook his head.

"You know something, Dutton." he remarked narrowing his eyes.

"You are a man full of surprises and I think you have a bright future in serving as a Priest. You certainly have the knack for it."

Dutton gave him a look of guarded offense.

"Well," Sir Almas paused to take a deep breath. "I suppose if I wish to put food on the table and clothes on our backs, then I must consider every option.

We have to discuss this possibility in length if you don't mind."

"Of course, not." Dutton readily agreed. "We can get started immediately, if you wish."

"No, we will wait until evening meal," Sir Almas quickly countered.

"I want both Della and Marie to be present. Whatever I am about to do, I wish for them to be fully aware of it and Della needs to be a part of my decision. For it will directly affect her."

"Of course, I understand completely." Dutton approved heartily. "As it should be."

"Good, very good." Sir Almas gave a slow nod. "Thank you, Dutton."

"Anytime." the young man said bowing his head.

"Shall we go in?" the knight invited.

Going ahead of Sir Almas, the two of them reentered the cottage. Sir Almas was left with much to consider.

With the helpful assistance of Dutton, Sir Almas was more easily able to go into the field in a position similar to a Sword-for-Hire and work as a private bodyguard for tradesmen and merchants passing through Oak Land. It wasn't exactly what the knight imagined he would end up doing for a living, but he was happy to have work all the same.

Sir Brutus Missiani was taken before King Théoden to stand trial for his crimes; Sir Almas, Priest Lumis, and Marie traveled to the kingdom of Ravens Burg to testify as witnesses against him. At the time, Della was left home in the care of Dutton, who Sir Almas was grateful had shown up when he did.

Della was comfortable around the young apprentice just as she was with Priest Lumis. When Sir Almas inquired about leaving Dutton to look after her, Della was in full agreement. When he inquired why, she told him that there was something about Dutton that made her feel relaxed around him and knew he could be trusted.

She told him that Dutton's eyes held a deep understanding and gentleness, something she had only seen in Sir Almas's eyes. Even though there was so much mystery about the apprentice Priest, Della knew he was of a special nature of person that was reliable.

Sir Missiani was placed in prison with a life sentence and his estate was broken up. His servants were given their freedom and went their own way out into the world. The coin that Sir Almas owed to Sir Missiani was to be given to the abbey to aid in the care of the other rescued women; and payable when the knight had the coin.

Marie as a free woman, knew that Della trusted her enough to feel safe in her company and liked being around Sir Almas, therefore she took up a job as the knight's housemaid.

Sir Almas also knew that having the elder woman around the house would silence anyone gossiping about him living in sin with Della. The knight never had any intentions of doing that, but he knew how much people loved to gossip and would target Della on purpose for being a Varamorean.

He knew she already had enough scrutiny to deal with, it didn't need to be added to.

When Sir Almas was away on a job, Della stayed at home with Marie caring for the house and doing daily chores. Sometimes, Sir Almas' work would take him away from home for days at a time, being away for prolonged periods of time caused him to worry about Della.

His worries were always put at ease when he would arrive home and Della would rush out of the front door to meet him. She was usually smiling and would hug him tightly before giving him a kiss. Having Della at home waiting for him to look forward to, made his new job all the easier.

He cherished the time they got to spend together.

Even in this, though, he knew that Della wasn't truly happy—nor did she feel safe. She hardly left the house even with someone accompanying her and would never go to the market. She barely spoke since the incident with Sir Missiani, and the knight felt that she probably never would.

He wasn't concerned if she never spoke much, he only wanted her to be happy and safe.

So far, though, she wasn't.

During his duties, the knight would inquire of those he worked for about places that would be ideal to move to. He let it be known that he was looking for a place that would be suitable for a Varamorean, somewhere where they were accepted.

Going over the many options, it seemed that there were only two viable places to move to.

Either to move to the far away kingdom of Brooklyn Falls in the mountains or to go to their sister kingdom, Delmar. Those were the only two places that were likely to accept someone like Della.

"Obviously, Brooklyn Falls would be an excellent choice. I have met the people from there and they are very kind, but the weather seems much too brutally cold."

He was explaining to Marie and Della one evening over supper.

"We could bear it, if we had to." Marie offered readily as she glanced over at Della who nodded.

"I have no doubt you would try—both of you." the knight said as he adamantly shook his head.

"No, it's far too cold and it would be cruel on all of us."

"How about Delmar?" Marie asked.

"That would be my best guess, only it might be difficult to fit in at first." Sir Almas said in a tone of warning.

"They are not accustomed to taking in outsiders. They aren't cruel people nor judgmental, but they tend to keep to themselves. We wouldn't have to worry about our safety either. They respect you as an equal."

Marie gave Della a small smile of encouragement and Della nodded visibly relieved at the news.

"What do you all think?"

"Whatever you decide, we will go along with." Marie reasoned.

"No," Sir Almas corrected firmly.

"You two are entitled to your own opinions; this decision will affect all of us."

Marie stared at the knight with speechless astonishment.

"Well?" Sir Almas asked patiently.

"I—I think I would be fine with any choice that is made, as long as I can stay in service to you." Marie answered still in shock.

"Good." the knight said nodding pleased as he looked over at Della.

"Della?" he asked softly.

Della hesitated, before she laid her spoon down beside her bowl and looked across the table at the knight.

"I care not where I go," she replied steadily. "Where you go, I go. I trust your every decision."

"It's settled then," Sir Almas announced.

"We will move to Delmar before Spring."

"Sir Almas," Marie asked with timid hesitation.

"Yes, Marie?" the knight said looking over at her.

"Can you tell us about our new home? I am from the kingdom of Sand Land originally and Della is of Varamor. We know nothing of the kingdom of Delmar or it's customs."

"I would be delighted to." Sir Almas said, a wide grin broke out on his face.

Just as he was about to begin, Della slid back her chair and stood up. The knight looked over at her, worried that something had upset her. Much to his surprise, the young woman walked around the table coming over to him.

Sir Almas turned toward her, unsure of what Della was up to. The young woman knelt beside his chair and laid her head in his lap. The knight was taken by surprise and slightly embarrassed by her actions.

Marie seemed unbothered by what the young woman had done and patiently waited for the knight to begin his talk about the kingdom of Delmar.

Taking a deep breath; Sir Almas laid a hand of comfort on Della's shoulder, before he launched into his description of their soon-to-be new home.

Chapter

40

"I AM CURIOUS, DELLA." SIR ALMAS BEGAN AS THEY TOOK their usual walk along the countryside.

"Yes," Della muttered as she held her dress skirt up slightly to keep it from dragging along the damp grass.

"How do you feel about learning to ride?" the knight offered.

"Ride? Why?" Della asked stopping short.

"It would be a tremendous help for when we move later. Then you could ride a horse of your own." Sir Almas proposed.

"I am not sure," Della stammered hesitantly. "I won't be any good."

"That's the point of teaching you." the knight remarked smiling with amusement.

"Well, I suppose it would be a fine idea." the young woman replied nodding.

"Good, then we can get started tomorrow after breakfast." the knight decided.

"Very well," Della acknowledged.

They walked along in silence until they arrived at the pond and open meadow. Della stopped at the entrance of the meadow and took in a deep breath. Sir Almas stopped beside her observing her and he noticed that she had tears trickling down her face.

"Della are you all right?" the knight asked gently touching her arm.

She sniffed and nodded.

"Why did you take me in and defend me?" she asked barely above a whisper.

The knight was puzzled by her question and when he did not reply, she turned her attention to him.

"I…" Sir Almas began slowly.

"I didn't know why at first, maybe it was out of pity. I do know that over time, the more I spent around you the more I figured out why." Della patiently waited for him to continue.

"When I was a young lad and my parents died, I put all regard for myself and my desires aside. I had to take care of my baby sister, Amelia. There was a position as a Page open to me by the council of Oak Land and I jumped at it. Ever since then, I based every decision I ever made on what others told me or that I believed was good for my sister.

It wasn't a dreadful thing at first, especially when Amelia was very small—I am her brother and owed it to her to care for her." Sir Almas insisted.

"But as I got older, I realized I never made any decisions for myself and missed many great opportunities because of it. I always based them off what my superiors and friends wanted.

And that all changed when I met you." Sir Almas paused gazing into her eyes with pleased compassion.

"When I took you in against Toby's advice, I made my first choice ever; based on my own feelings. I made it for you—and myself."

Della was perplexed by what Sir Almas was trying to convey.

"You, Della gave me my independence back. My backbone, essentially." Sir Almas revealed.

"I have for the first time in a long time, learned how to love. I thought my love and true happiness died with my parents and I cared for Amelia out of responsibility…not love.

I am ashamed to admit it, but it's the truth. I didn't believe in love—I was convinced that it was mythical or foolish hope. But then I met you…and you changed all of that."

Della's mouth slightly dropped open and she stared at Sir Almas with admiration and surprise. He had revealed something very personal to her, that helped her understand his attitude and actions regarding her.

"But why me?" Della couldn't help asking. "I am spoiled… damaged goods."

Deep down, she felt unworthy of the knight's love—as well as anyone else's, especially after what Sir Missiani had done to her. Ever since the incident it had driven somewhat of a wedge between her and Sir Almas.

She felt too ashamed to look into his face when she was speaking to him or when he spoke to her. Even when he touched her, she wanted to flinch away and bid him not to touch her because she was not good enough.

Della frowned lowering her gaze as fresh tears welled in her eyes, feeling a tremendous amount of shame come over her.

"No," Sir Almas countered stepping in front of her and lifted her chin. She looked into his eyes with her tear-filled soft brown ones.

His gaze reflected tender compassion and love.

"No, that's not true. You are not what others try to make you. *You*, Della, are strong, brave, and beautiful. I am honored to call you my own.

I am very blessed to have someone like you in my life." Sir Almas said meaning every word. "I am a better man because of you."

"But having me here is causing you so much strife and trouble. Maybe it would have been best if I never came." the young woman reasoned closing her eyes, not being able to look into the knight's sympathetic gaze.

"And deprive me of my only possible chance of finding love and the opportunity to be truly happy?"

"What of your family and career? All that has been changed because of me."

"No, I needed a career change. Being a knight for this kingdom isn't everything I always thought it would be. Instead of serving for honor and valor, they only want personal glory and loot. The injury that I suffered in the games would have happened regardless of you being around or not, perhaps it was just God's way of forcing me to realize it was time to move on." Sir Almas replied bitterly, his face twisting into a frown of distaste.

"As for Amelia and Toby—they don't dictate my life nor choose whom I am to love. They are choosing to be bitter and angry when they have no reason to be. You have to remember to pay them no mind."

"But I have made life hard for you and you have to move because of me." Della remarked feeling guilty.

"It doesn't matter," the knight chuckled easily. "I want you to be happy and feel safe wherever we choose to call home. No matter where we have to go or where we end up having to live. Anywhere is fine with me, as long as I have you."

"You are my happiness and my home."

Hearing this made Della open her eyes and look up at the knight and slowly smiled. All the apprehension and guilt she was feeling began to ebb away.

"As you are mine." Della whispered smiling at him.

"We make decisions for each other from now on, right?" Sir Almas inquired.

"Yes," Della replied wrapping her arms around the knight.

"Forever and always."

"Always," Sir Almas muttered warmly embracing Della.

"I have never loved anyone as much as I love you now."

Della felt herself blush under the knight's gentle gaze, feeling honored by Sir Almas's confession of love to her.

Leaning down the knight planted a soft kiss on her lips.

Chapter

41

OVER THE COURSE OF THE NEXT FEW WEEKS Della and Sir Almas spent time getting to know more about each other. With trial and error, Della eventually learned to ride horse and became such a good horse woman that she even rivaled Sir Almas's skills.

Gradually, Della went back to her happy smiling self and went to market, but only with Sir Almas close. People stared at them when they were out among the villagers; no doubt judging Sir Almas for being with a former slave and a Varamorean. But Sir Almas paid them no attention, he was happy and so was his Della, and that is all that mattered as far as he was concerned.

Della found pure happiness and joy that she had never known before. She was so happy, that at times she was able to forget about all the horrible things that had been done to her. Sometimes, the terrible memories returned to her in frightening nightmares.

When she would wake up trembling and screaming; Sir Almas would come rushing into her room. He would sit on the edge of her bed and hold onto her until she calmed down and fell back to sleep. The bad memories she knew she could never forget, but she wasn't going to allow them to hold her back.

Della knew that the people of Oak Land were hard on Sir Almas because he made the choice to love her. Della tried her hardest not to let it bother her and do as Sir Almas told her. Still, it got difficult at times and she wasn't sure all the suffering and heartache was worth it.

When she would be welcoming Sir Almas home after a long day or week of Sword-for-Hire work, she was reminded of why it was worth it. The knight had become someone that she could trust absolutely and feel safe with being around.

She knew deep down in her heart that Sir Almas would be the only person she would ever trust for as long as she lived. Everyone else that she had ever met used her or broke her trust. Only the knight had been different; he had fought for her when no one else had. With the knight, Della felt that trust and love was the most important things between them.

"I heard from my sister today." Sir Almas told her as they walked toward the house together.

Sir Almas had a hand slung around her shoulders; Della was leaning into him and held onto his one hand.

"Oh," Della acknowledged feeling uneasy.

"Well, not her precisely," Sir Almas corrected himself. "A messenger brought a note over from her."

"Is everything well with her and Toby?" Della asked expressing her concern.

"Yes, she's just fine—as is Toby." the knight reassured her.

"What was the note about?" the young woman ventured with pretended interest.

Della really did not want to have anything to do with Amelia and Captain Toby—nor did she care about what they did.

"It was an invitation to their wedding." Sir Almas said glancing down to see what her reaction would be.

"She's finally getting married?" Della asked a little surprised. "And they have invited us?"

"Yes,"

"Will you go?"

"I am her brother and it's expected of me." Sir Almas replied sounding slightly unenthused.

"I see." Della said nodding.

"But I won't go unless you go with me and I can escort you."

"No, I cannot." Della refused.

"Come on, Della you can't let the past bother you." the knight pleaded.

"Show everyone how strong and resilient you are by coming with me."

"No, I won't create an issue for you—it's not my place." as she said this, Della pulled away from the knight abruptly.

"Go and be there for your sister and show your blessing on her marriage to Toby. Don't worry about me; I will be here with Marie."

"Della," Sir Almas began to reason.

Della countered by shaking her head firmly, she backed away quickly and turned hurrying away.

Why does she have to be like this? I thought we resolved all the issues between them and us. Sir Almas thought in frustration as he watched her disappear into the house.

Well, I have three weeks to convince her to come with me.

For the next three days he was unsuccessful in mentioning anything about the wedding, because Della refused to hear of it. Whenever he tried to bring it up, she would only walk away.

Amelia and Toby's attitude and treatment of the young woman really had a negative effect on Della. For some reason, Sir Almas found that he was bothered by this, and deep down he wanted Della to be accepted by his family most of all. Toby and Amelia would have to learn to see Della as part of their family, now that the knight was starting to court her.

This wedding is a perfect opportunity for our relationship to be out in the open. Sir Almas continuously convinced himself.

By day four, Sir Almas was running short of patience with Della's stubborn behavior and decided to confront her about it.

He did so on their daily walk.

"Why won't you come with me?" Sir Almas demanded.

"I told you many times already, that I don't want to hear about it." Della replied paying him no mind as they walked along.

"Why? Just tell me why?" the knight challenged pulling her to a stop.

Della stopped and turned to him her face was flush and eyes in a hard glare.

"Because I can't stand being surrounded by people who pass judgement on me because of where I come from!" Della snapped.

"I notice the stares, sneers, and low mutters when people look at us and point. They hate me for who I am and you because you care for me.

Why would I show my face at a gathering where we would be the odd ones?"

The knight stared at her with sympathy and sorrow, fully understanding Della's feelings toward social gatherings and his family."

"Oh, Della, I am so sorry." the knight apologized feeling guilty.

"Your people only know hatred for anyone that is different from them. They cannot open their minds and be accepting or learn to forgive!" Della shouted in fury.

"You try to teach me to forgive all who have wronged me all my life, but why should I when your own people can't?"

"Because it's what Jesus does!" Sir Almas refuted.

"He forgives us each and every day, whether or not we deserve it. Therefore, I have tried to strive to be as He is."

"Why does He forgive?" the young woman asked in frustration.

"Because He loves us unconditionally."

"How?"

"He just does, He himself is love—He is incapable of hate. He can only love and forgive.

And we should try to follow his example and try to be as He is."

"It's easy for you to say because you know Him, but I do not."

"Would you want to learn?" Sir Almas asked hopefully.

"Over time…yes," Della said nodding. "Perhaps, if I could know more about your God, then I can understand why we should forgive."

"I have many…that I cannot forgive, but maybe I—I can learn to try."

"Yes, you will." Sir Almas said encouragingly. "When you know Jesus, you will feel little to no anger and understanding forgiveness will make more sense."

"I hope so," Della said sighing deeply.

"Trust me, you will." the knight said earnestly.

"So, will you go to my sister's wedding with me?"

"I—I," Della struggled hating the very idea of being surrounded by people who hated her.

"If it becomes too hard for you to bear, then we will leave the event early." Sir Almas reasoned one last time.

"You can come up at anytime and tell me during the wedding if you need to leave. I promise you that I will take you away from there."

"I am not sure." Della hesitated.

"Please, just give it a chance." Sir Almas begged.

Della's shoulders sagged and she let out a heaving sigh before she slowly gave a nod.

"Yes, for you I will." Della gave in resignedly.

"Thank you," the knight said gratefully, he let out a relieved breath and visibly relaxed.

"Thank-you for agreeing to go. If you had said no, I would not have gone.

I couldn't have."

"You could have, she is your sister." Della countered adamantly.

"No," Sir Almas rejected sternly.

"It wouldn't feel the same without you. I would feel incomplete."

Della gave the knight a hard look to be sure he meant what he said. By the look in his eyes, she knew he meant every word.

"You complete me, Della." Sir Almas offered his hands to her.

Della willingly took them, and the knight lowered himself to one knee before her.

"I do not want to be alone anymore, but for us to be part of the same body. Husband and wife, if you'll have me."

The young woman gasped in stunned surprise at the knight's heartfelt proposal. She stood there grasping his hands; feeling warmth and pure joy run through her. She knew for certain that she wanted what the knight asked for.

Della found that she could not form the words in her mouth as she became choked up, but she gave a vigorous nod of her head. The knight rose to his feet and pulled Della towards him into an embrace.

"I will stay true to you forever and always." he promised her before he kissed her lovingly.

"Never to stray."

"I will always love you," Della whispered looking up into his gentle loving eyes. "I will love only you. Forever and always. Never to stray."

Sir Almas felt a swell of pride deep down in his chest as he held the woman he passionately loved in his arms.

"My love," he told her drinking in all her beauty.

The young woman never felt more in love in all her life as she gazed at the knight.

"When I have a little coin, I shall buy you a proper ring, to make this official." Sir Almas told her.

Della could see in his eyes that he was feeling rather terrible about not having a ring to present to the woman he intended to make his wife.

"It does not matter," Della assured him. "We have each other and that's all that is important."

The knight couldn't help, but love her all the more for this.

Suddenly a thought occurred to him.

My ring of knighthood to Oak Land! he thought.

Bringing his hands up before Della, he pulled the ring from his right middle finger. The ring was largely oversized for Della's small delicate hands; it was a faded coppery metal with the oak tree on a hill, the crest of the kingdom of Oak Land.

"Here," he announced slipping it upon her delicate thin ring finger.

"This shall suffice for now."

Della was so overcome with joy that she began to sob out of admiration for the knight's ring.

"It's perfect," she said gazing at the symbol and pledge of their love.

"As you are." Sir Almas said lifting her face towards him.

He bent his head down and gave her a long loving kiss.

Della…my soon-to-be wife. he reflected feeling blissful.

Chapter

42

ELLA AND SIR ALMAS WERE WED IN A PRIVATE ceremony later that week with only Priest Lumis and Marie in attendance. What made the time even more memorable was that the Priest brought the good news that the council of Oak Land finally decided that the young woman could stay under the knight's care.

They had heard and seen of all the good that being with the knight had done for the young woman and the council felt that she had been reformed enough to join the ranks of society. After the incident with Sir Missiani, the council knew without a doubt that the young woman was better off in the care of Sir Almas.

Both Della and Sir Almas were overjoyed at this news and took it as a cue to get married.

Sir Almas offered to have a fitted ring forged to her size, but Della simply refused. She said that Sir Almas' ring of knighthood was more special because it had been a part of their lives since meeting. Even though the ring was much too large for her tiny finger; Della wore it proudly around her neck on a leather cord.

We belong to each other now. she mused as she rubbed her fingers over the ring that hung around her neck.

She gazed lovingly at Sir Almas who was busily stoking the fireplace and putting more wood in it. Della noticed, as she often had, that though Sir Almas appeared strong and cold; he had a softer side. A side that most people rarely ever saw, a side that he showed only to those whom he loved and cared about.

Della saw the rare eclipse of his gentle loving side when they first encountered each other almost a year ago. At the time she held onto such hatred and denial that she never believed that anyone could be kind to her.

But at the point that she knew his intentions were true was when he was willing to let her go.

When you know someone genuinely loves you and you love them, you will know when you can let them go. It was something that she remembered her father told her, the only thing she could recall from him.

Love is a fragile thing which must be nurtured so that it will flourish.
"What?" Sir Almas asked with amusement as he looked up at her.

"Nothing," Della replied giving a little shrug.

"You're smiling at me with that dreamy look you sometimes have," the knight remarked straightening up.

"What are you thinking about, love?"

"The day we met," the young woman replied closing her eyes for a moment.

"Hmm," Sir Almas muttered with satisfaction. "I remember."

"I never imagined we would be where we are now. That I could or would ever be someone's wife."

"Ah, but you are mine," Sir Almas said smiling warmly.

"And I wouldn't want it any other way." Della added.

"Well, are you ready for tomorrow?" Sir Almas asked becoming quite somber.

"I don't think I could ever be, but with you at my side I know I will be brave enough to make it through it." Della said positively.

"You have always been a very brave woman."

"It helps greatly to have you, because you are a pillar for me to hold onto when all I want to do is flee." Della said heartfeltly.

"I have firmly decided that I am going to forgive your sister—and Toby. I don't want any bad blood between us on account of my anger towards them."

"Forgive Amelia and Toby for what? You've never done anything to them." Sir Almas challenged puzzled.

"No, not to their faces—but in my heart I have hated them." Della confessed lowering her head. "I know that God is the only one who knows what's in my heart and that I feel guilty about my thoughts against them."

Raising her head bravely, Della took a deep breath and gave the knight a firm gaze.

"Through my newfound faith in God, I want to leave all my old ways behind, which means finding a way to forgive those who wronged me.

Which I have—in my heart for all those who are no longer around or a part of my life. All who remain to forgive are Amelia, Toby, and...and Sir M—Missiani."

Della squeezed her eyes shut tightly and shuttered at the mention of the man's name who took advantage of her.

"Brutus does not deserve forgiveness." the knight muttered coldly under his breath.

"Perhaps not, but it's something that I must do in order to find peace," Della reasoned solemnly.

"He will be the most difficult—and I am not ready to forgive him yet, for I harbor so much anger and hatred for him."

"If it is something you must do, then you will have to do it in your own time," the knight encouraged with understanding.

"This, I must do." Della insisted nodding. "I am ready to forgive Amelia and Toby—then maybe we will have a chance at being a family."

I hope so too," Sir Almas agreed although he felt it would be unlikely, at least not right away.

If ever, considering how long his family could hold a grudge.

Some people could often harbor grudges for years, to even a lifetime. Sadly, Amelia was one such person who held onto things; she wasn't a believer in forgiveness or the Lord as her brother was. She was not one to forgive and forget easily, there was too much water under that bridge.

But Della's hope was a good one of pure intentions and if God willed it, then anything was possible. Still, Sir Almas had strong doubts that their relationship could be reconciled so quickly and easily.

Chapter

43

MELIA'S WEDDING WAS UPSCALE WITH NEARLY A hundred guests in attendance. It was held in a lavish white stone mansion house that belonged to one of Captain Toby's cousins that was a council member of the kingdom. The windows, door frames, and rails of the house were decorated with strings of multi-colored flowers.

Rose pedals were cast all around on every floor of the big house. A merry musical band played in one corner of the feasting hall, while people danced and ate.

Amelia and Captain Toby sat behind a small table at the head of the room. The guests were arriving to the celebration ball and greeted the couple as they entered the hall. Amelia was dressed in a long flowing off-white dress with a low neckline with ruffled edging shaped like flowers. Captain Toby wore his ceremonial Oak Land armor that was shiny silver with a rich green tunic and cloak.

The women and men wore fancy brightly colored clothes. Everyone was in good spirits after the wedding ceremony, laughing, eating and dancing merrily about.

Sir Almas had gifted Della with a new dress and shoes for the wedding. The dress was a long gown, with a low V-neck, and golden lace around the bodice. It was a rich maroon red and there were red slippers to match.

Della wore the first new dress that belonged to her with pride.

She was going to put her long black hair into her usual braid, but Sir Almas had other plans. He let her hair loose, combing it straight, he pulled it all to one side, so it hung over one shoulder. Sir Almas then placed a clip adorned with silver and white beads in her hair to keep it to the side and out of her eyes.

"Perfect," he admired stepping back to observe his handiwork.

"Your hair is a natural beauty that should be shared."

"Thank you," Della nodded gratefully.

"Let's be off," he said offering his arm to her.

Della took his arm; his palm was turned upward, and she laid hers down on top of his and laced her fingers through his. Gazing lovingly into her eyes, the knight had to lean over and give her a peck on the cheek.

"You look breathtaking," he told her.

Della just laid her head onto his shoulder and patted his chest with her hand. He was making her feel embarrassed with all the attention and praise.

When Della and Sir Almas came striding through the entrance into the mansion, all eyes were on them. Everyone stopped doing what they had been before Sir Almas and Della had entered the room.

They stared and a deafening silence engulfed the whole room.

With eyes locked on them; Della could feel their cruel wordless judgements being passed on them. She felt fearful panic welling up in her chest and she began to instinctively pull back.

All she wanted to do was to run.

Suddenly, Sir Almas laid his other hand over the top of hers and patted it with comforting encouragement. This brought Della back to reality and knowing that Sir Almas was right at her side, made her feel better.

She leaned closer to him, where she felt protected.

Captain Toby gave them a stiff frown as they approached the table. Amelia could not mask the look of shock and pure anger she was feeling at the very sight of Della.

"Congratulations on your blessed day," Sir Almas addressed bowing his head as he stood before them.

"Amelia and Captain Toby Falkner, I wish you many years of blessings and happiness."

Sir Almas gave his sister a timid warm smile, holding a handout to her. Della knew that her husband was hopeful that his sister would allow him to kiss her hand; if she did, then he knew their relationship could be redeemed.

"What is *she* doing here?" Amelia asked icily as she glared at Della.

"She's here because she is my wife," Sir Almas replied firmly. "She's family."

At the news that they were husband and wife; Amelia gave her brother a startled look and her cheeks flushed red from anger.

"Not mine," his sister sneered bitterly pressing her lips together.

"How dare you bring her here and flaunt her around. She's not one of us—she doesn't belong."

Sir Almas straightened up; taken aback by Amelia's cold harsh behavior.

"She has as much right to be here as anyone else!" Sir Almas hissed through clenched teeth.

"She does not, Almas." Captain Toby corrected. "She's a Varamorean and she will never be an Oak Lander."

"You—" Sir Almas hissed.

"Almas, no," Della whispered laying a hand of restraint on his chest, half turning toward him.

"Be the better man, forgive even if it is hard. No bad blood, remember?"

Sir Almas slightly relaxed, rocking back and forth on his heels. He bit his lip as if to hold back everything he wanted to say.

"Toby, Amelia." Della addressed them giving them curt nods. "I wish you all the joys and happy years as husband and wife.

Know that I harbor no ill will or hatred toward you both and forgive you both for everything you have said against me and may do again."

"Forgiveness?!" Amelia scoffed throwing her head back.

"Why would I want your forgiveness? It is tainted."

"Then I feel pity for you, because if you never learn to forgive, your heart will be filled with bitterness and you will not know true peace. Not until you begin to forgive." Della said gravely.

"Ha! What do you know?" Amelia muttered with vile.

"Your words mean nothing slave...wench."

"That's enough, Amelia!" Sir Almas jumped in defensively.

"That's lowly—even for you."

Amelia shot her brother an offended look, as though he should not have said anything.

"Why don't you two leave before you cause any more trouble." Captain Toby said, his tone filled with annoyance.

"I wish things could have been different between us," Sir Almas said his tone full of hurt.

"But now...now I know we don't have a chance to patch things up."

Both Captain Toby and Amelia gave Sir Almas perplexed looks.

"I don't think we shall see each other again. Good-bye."

Della could feel how tense Sir Almas was, one look in his eyes and she could see the heartbreak he was being put through. She gave his hand a gentle squeeze trying to comfort him somehow.

They strode quickly out of the mansion; the knight sucked in a deep shuttering breath once they were outside and the door was closed behind them. In the bluish-twilight Della could see the tears glistening in his eyes. Her heart hurt for him knowing that he had to watch his family fall apart—to lose his sister.

"I am sorry," Della apologized feeling somehow responsible.

"What?" Sir Almas stopped abruptly and faced her.

"I am sorry about everything that has happened." Della replied.

"What—why are you sorry?" he asked puzzled and shocked.

"You have lost your family," Della said her voice scarcely above a whisper. "Because of me."

The knight shook his head and looked away for a moment before he looked back at her.

"My family...Della," he said smiling blissfully at her.

"My family is you. You're everything to me."

"What about Amelia, she's your sister?"

"She is, but she has made the choice not to be a family anymore when she refused to accept you." the knight explained. "You are my family. We don't need people like them in our life."

"You're doing this for me?" Della asked with uncertainty.

"For us," the knight reaffirmed grasping her hands in his.

"The kingdom of Delmar and our new home awaits us. Let us start the next chapter in our lives, let us create our own family.

Leave this life behind and everyone in it!"

Della stared at the knight surprised by his eager declaration.

"A—are you sure?" Della asked hesitantly.

"Yes, I am ready for it." the knight assured her.

"Let us do it, then." Della said as a smile spread over her face.

"Make our own family."

The knight pulled her towards him and lifted her off her feet, spinning around in a circle. They were both laughing in carefree delight.

"We can have children. How about five...no, ten!" Sir Almas rambled excitedly.

"Ten?" Della giggled at his almost child-like eagerness. "A bit much? How shall we ever manage such a large family?"

"Simple," the knight stated in a matter-of-fact tone.

"The way we always have. By faith."

Della smiled gazing into the eyes of the man she loved deeply; her heart swelled with love and she felt immense peace.

"With faith forever." Della whispered as she leaned down, and their lips met.

She believed it too.

Through a broken life, dreams, and trust—she found faith and peace again. God brought the knight into her life and they helped each other heal and find their own independence.

Faith was the beauty in both of their shattered dreams.

"We will create new dreams; God will be at the center of it—and our hope." he told her as he held her in his arms, her head resting on his chest, while they rocked back and forth.

They found love in each other.

Epilogue

Sir Almas and Della moved to the kingdom of Delmar. Here the people accepted them more easily, though it took a year for them to fully settle in. Many of the residents of Delmar had come from the land of Varamor themselves and Della did not feel so out of place among them.

Sir Almas worked as a Sword-for-Hire for several months after coming to Delmar. They moved into a small cottage home in the countryside and Della raised a small flock of sheep for wool, meat, and milk.

One day, Sir Almas was approached by a Horse Commander of the army of Delmar. He was offered the position among them to serve as a combat instructor for young squires in training. Sir Almas asked Della what her thoughts were on him regarding the position, she told him that the choice was his completely.

After days of careful thought and research, Sir Almas found that the kingdom still strove to serve the people with honor and justice—something he had always hoped and dreamed of.

To him the decision was an easy, yes.

Sir Almas found a renewed joy in being an instructor and sharing his knowledge with the young squires. His arm was never strong enough to carry a sword, but it was of little consequence when he was training young lads.

The people of Delmar came to accept and cherish the Martin's over time. Della was surrounded by men and women who saw her as an equal. Many people relied on Sir Almas for friendship and good advice.

Life was good for Della and Sir Almas in the kingdom of Delmar.

Marie ended up staying in the kingdom of Oak Land, where she served Priest Lumis for a time as his maid, and eventually the two of them married. They would plan a trip once a year to come to the kingdom of Delmar to visit Sir Almas and Della.

When they were settled for two years, Della and Sir Almas started on their family.

Della gave birth to her first son, whom they named Zander and their second son born nearly six years later was named Christopher.

The boys were showered with love and taught valuable wholesome life lessons.

Della and Sir Almas could not fathom at the time how important their two boys would become. Or that they were destined to play a vital role in the future of the land of Teary Isles, that would change the fabric of things to come forever after.

About the Author

P. Dutton, author of Tales of Teary Isles: Beauty in the Shattered spends much of their time on their family's farm in rural, Hitterdal, Minnesota, caring for horses, sheep, and dogs where much of the inspiration for stories like this comes from.

Printed in the United States
by Baker & Taylor Publisher Services